Down
in the
Ground

Essential Prose Series 180

 Canada Council   Conseil des Arts
for the Arts   du Canada

 ONTARIO ARTS COUNCIL
CONSEIL DES ARTS DE L'ONTARIO
an Ontario government agency
un organisme du gouvernement de l'Ontario

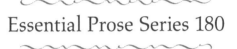

Guernica Editions Inc. acknowledges the support of the Canada Council for the Arts and the Ontario Arts Council. The Ontario Arts Council is an agency of the Government of Ontario.

We acknowledge the financial support of the Government of Canada.

Down in the Ground

Bruce Meyer

**GUERNICA
EDITIONS**
TORONTO · CHICAGO · BUFFALO · LANCASTER (U.K.)
2020

Copyright © 2020, Bruce Meyer and Guernica Editions Inc.
All rights reserved. The use of any part of this publication,
reproduced, transmitted in any form or by any means, electronic,
mechanical, photocopying, recording or otherwise stored
in a retrieval system, without the prior consent
of the publisher is an infringement of the copyright law.

Michael Mirolla, editor
David Moratto, interior and cover design
Guernica Editions Inc.
287 Templemead Drive, Hamilton (ON), Canada L8W 2W4
2250 Military Road, Tonawanda, N.Y. 14150-6000 U.S.A.
www.guernicaeditions.com

Distributors:
Independent Publishers Group (IPG)
600 North Pulaski Road, Chicago IL 60624
University of Toronto Press Distribution,
5201 Dufferin Street, Toronto (ON), Canada M3H 5T8
Gazelle Book Services, White Cross Mills
High Town, Lancaster LA1 4XS U.K.

First edition.
Printed in Canada.
Legal Deposit—Third Quarter
Library of Congress Catalog Card Number: 2019949234
Library and Archives Canada Cataloguing in Publication
Title: Down in the ground / Bruce Meyer.
Names: Meyer, Bruce, 1957- author.
Series: Essential prose series ; 180.
Description: First edition. | Series statement:
Essential prose series ; 180 | Short stories.
Identifiers: Canadiana (print) 20190176156 |
Canadiana (ebook) 20190176164 | ISBN 9781771834889 (softcover) |
ISBN 9781771834896 (EPUB) | ISBN 9781771834902 (Kindle)
Classification: LCC PS8576.E93 D69 2020 | DDC C813/.54—dc23

Contents

THE END
- Down in the Ground 3
- The Wildflowers of Ontario 9
- In Place 13
- Restoration 23
- Empty 31
- Star of Wonder 35
- Cadenza 41
- A Month of Good Luck 45
- The Smell of Spring 49
- Consuelo 55
- Looking Good 57

THE MIDDLE
- The Muse 63
- Alabaster 67
- The Tiptoe Effect 69
- The Warm-Up 73
- How to Fold a Letter 75
- When We Are Not Here 77
- Labour Day Monday 81
- Hoodie 87

Snow Pudding 93
Leash 97
Top Six. 99
What Kasha Said 105
The Sophomore Philosophy Club 111
The Run 115
Warts 121
Edible Flowers 123
Popcorn 127
Rec Room 133

THE BEGINNING

Ear to the Ground 143
The Higgins 147
Knowledge 151
Constant 159
Monster 165
Sadness 171
Racket 177
Providence 183
Sheet Music 187
Gift 191
Toll 197
Tentacle 199
Bicycle Bell 203
The Fishers 207

Acknowledgements 211
About the Author 213

*There are a thousand ways to kneel and kiss the ground;
there are a thousand ways to go home again.*
—**Rumi**

The foot feels the foot when it feels the ground.
—**Buddha**

*In dwelling, live close to the ground.
In thinking, keep to the simple.
In conflict, be fair and generous.
In governing, don't try to control.
In work, do what you enjoy.
In family life, be completely present.*
—**Lao Tzu**

THE END

Down in the Ground

MINERS DON'T COME up singing from the pit at the end of the day as they do in the movies. The older members of the family always pointed that out when they watched the old films about hardship and drama down in the ground. Men came up exhausted. As a tribute to their heritage, the family kept two Victorian bird cages and a newer cage purchased from a big-box pet store as reminders of where they had come from.

The larger of the two antique cages was a keepsake brought from the family's old country town near Bolsover. It was ornate brass. The bars were almost far enough apart for a bird to slip through, though not quite. The latch on the door was decorated in scroll work, and from a hook that dangled from the cupola hung a wire swing that was sleeved with a wooden cuff. Over the years, the perch cylinder had been sanded so that it was thin now and hard for a bird to wrap its claws around. By today's standards it wasn't a useful cage for a canary, but long ago it was tradition to keep a trilling canary in the house to brighten everyone's spirits during the day. If the bird sang at night, however, the music was an ill omen. Someone was going to die.

The second cage, a box made of forged wrought iron

rods, held a more ominous story. It sat on the mantel. The cage had survived the mines. It had been carried down in the ground by a great grandfather who worked the coal seams of the English Midlands before immigrating to Canada. Early each morning, the men of the town would file out the laneway doors of their cramped back yards and head up the hill to the shaft. A huge wheel stood at the pit-head where wooden-gated elevators of men in work clothes were lowered into the earth at the beginning of the day, and if they were lucky, were raised up at the end of a twelve-hour shift looking as if they had come from the fires of hell, the whites of their eyes round, empty, and exhausted. They carried their pickaxes and oil lamps in one hand and their iron cages and canary in the other. They had lived another day to feed their families.

The great-grandfather, and generations before him, must have dug every square inch of coal from the darkness of the deep below their town because the old mine collapsed one morning and swallowed the streets, houses, shops, banks, churches, and graveyards where the family had lived and died and been buried long before anyone began recording the history of the place. Their heritage sank into the abyss as if the ground was time itself, cloaking, impenetrable, and silent. "That is what becomes of the past, of work, love, life, and even death," some of the family elders said. "It all goes down in the ground."

A newspaper clipping in a book on the shelf next to the mantel, a fragile, yellowing scrap of paper torn from a Midlands tabloid, described how there had been a rumbling, a moaning as if the earth was giving its last gasp, and then the town was gone to the sound of walls falling, windows shattering, and pianos crashing to their last notes. Local authorities erected a fence around the area and rerouted the roads—roads had led there long before the Doomsday Book. A photograph in the article showed several of the row houses leaning and tipped into the earth. One address was almost intact, as if it had simply put itself down for a nap, never to wake again. A lace curtain hung out through the glass of a broken window like the tongue of a battered boxer or a cartoon character who has x's where his dead eyes used to be.

When the town collapsed, several of the older family members said it was a shame the government had placed mechanical detectors in the caverns instead of live canaries. The canaries would have been more reliable. Lives could have been saved. Canaries not only warned miners of poisonous gas build-up: if the birds stopped singing it was also the sign of an impending collapse. But who would have looked after the creatures? Who would be brave enough or fool enough to go down in the ground each day and bring the birds back to the surface while sending others down in their place? There is no fury like the hell beneath us, they said. Even when we are alive and walking through our homes or meadows or streets, they proffered, we are walking on our own graves. That is the reality no one wants to acknowledge, they said. Once, long ago, we knew the past but have forgotten it today. Government officials said the birds were unreliable, antique icons of a mythology of labour in an era when dying was the way people made their living.

Mining families, such as the great-grandmother's, bred birds for their ability to sing, even in the dank and lightless confines of a coal seam. That art had been lost. The newer varieties of canaries came from breeding factories in Germany. The new ones were delicate pets, not working companions who gave their lives so that others might live. The pit birds were born to sing, and if the singing stopped, they died for their living. The sound of the pick axes striking the walls of black rock made the birds want to sing even harder. They were meant to inspire the miners the way a piper inspires soldiers in a battle.

It was a hard life, the mother told her children, when they asked why the family always had canaries. Everything about coal, their mother told them, was black. Their great-grandfather had died of black lung. If it was a child's duty to stoke the furnace on a winter night, his hands would be black when he emerged from the basement. Even the yellow canaries that their ancestors carried down in the ground would emerge sooty. Their fabled great-grandfather, the immigrant to Canada, had been through five canaries from his boyhood until he joined up to fight in the war. Three of them had died when the shafts gassed up. One had caught a cold in a draft because canaries are delicate no matter how broad their chests or how powerful their song. The other had died of sorrow when he went away to fight in the war.

The family always kept a canary in the house, not just as a reminder of the past but because they could not remember a time when there wasn't one among them. The current pet, Pavarotti, had a broad chest for a canary. He was bright yellow and was approaching the age of twelve. He was still loud enough to be heard on the other side of the street. Those who passed the house on summer days when the windows were open often stopped to listen and try to figure out where the bird was singing. Pavarotti didn't live in the iron canary box or in the elaborate brass cage. He had a newer model cage with a cuttlebone clipped to the side bars and a plastic swing he never sat on. His door was always open, but he never left his cage. The world inside the bars was his own territory. If someone put their hand in the cage, Pavarotti would attack it. Each canary—and only the males sang—had his own personality, and possessed a strange sense that their work was important. They responded to their owners, hopping up to the bars for a piece of grape or eating from the miner's hand when he held a smidgen of seed for them.

By late winter, Pavarotti was not well. He hadn't been well for several weeks. His once powerful song had diminished to a disconsolate chirp, then a hoarse croak. Canaries rarely live that long, the mother told her children. They waited and watched. They knew what would happen but nothing in the children's lives had ever been that fragile. Nothing had ever left them unexpectedly. They had been too young to remember the deaths of their grandparents. Those faces were simply unexplained absences.

On the morning that the mother reached into the bottom corner of the cage just beneath the open door, Pavarotti was breathing heavily. His body was puffed out. He hadn't the strength to fight her. She wrapped her hands around the bird, raised his beak to her lips and blew gently into his nostrils. She stroked his body, tapping his heart rhythmically with the speed at which it had always beat, and for a moment he opened his eyes. The children looked at each other and beamed. Their mother had worked a miracle. Then the bird struggled and his eyes closed.

The children cried. The boy thought that his mother might have murdered their pet—after all, the bird had predated their own lives—he had always been part of their world, a presence, a fact. And now the cage was empty.

That evening, the family gathered around a hole the boy had dug in the backyard. It was the first time he had wielded a heavy spade, and as he dug the hole he pictured himself as a miner, hauling up the rocks from the earth that would fuel a flame and warm the family; indeed, the early evening sun was warm on his skin. His sister had given the bird a handkerchief that had been a gift from an aunt. The green Victorian silk was stitched with tiny bluebirds. Pavarotti was laid in a coffee can and the lid was sealed shut. The boy knelt and laid the can in the earth.

The father bent down, and from a brown paper bag that had sat for an eternity on his workbench, and before that on the grandfather's workbench, emptied a black powder into the hole. It was the last of grains of a piece of coal the immigrant ancestor had carried with him to remind him of the home he left behind.

"Ashes to ashes, dust to dust. Ashes from the past," the father said. "And dust for the future."

He took the bird's body and, kneeling beside the deep hole he had dug in the garden, the boy said: "Be with your fellows now, good bird." Then reached into the darkness and set the tiny body among the drowned voices and sweet songs down in the ground.

The Wildflowers of Ontario

DAVID LOVED TO describe his childhood Sundays. They were not church Sundays, as was the case with some of the kids he grew up with. His days began slowly. He loved to search for words about the way sunlight would enter the kitchen at various times of the year while his father stood at the black and white tile counter and sectioned a grapefruit as if he was a cartographer drawing the full world for the first time. His mother would be at the stove, lifting the lid on the waffle iron or scrambling the eggs with a metal spatula.

Time had nowhere to go on those mornings, no matter what the season, and it lingered so that every detail of the placemats, the lily of the valley dishes with the green rims, the smell of coffee in the percolator, bubbling as the shots bounced against the glass dome—even the faint hum of the electric kitchen clock on the plaster drop above the sink and the green and yellow linoleum squares of the floor that Saskatchewan reminded him of the first time he flew over it—everything had a place and purpose in his mind.

Just after noon, they would drive over to his grandparents' house to pick them up and take them out for air in the country in their big four-door sedan. The dashboard was chrome. The seats were woven brown-and-black vinyl with white crestings on top, and the window handles had black knobs that spun in David's hands.

When they reached the outskirts of the city, his father would turn down the first dirt sideroad they could find. If it was summer, they would roll down the windows, reduce their speed so dust wouldn't fly inside the car, and cut the ignition when they reached an emptiness that wanted to speak to them. David would hear the grasshoppers in the scrub growth, the crickets chirping in the late August heat, and the songs of meadow birds. He even heard a hummingbird's wings as they stood beside the car with the engine off and the bird approached his grandmother who smelled of rose perfume.

His grandmother would gather wildflowers. When she was young, she had learned to press flowers, to keep them beyond their brief moments of bloom, though their colours would fade, and they would grow brittle: and yet, despite the laws of entropy, she would slow the force of time with her magic. She could stop the world from changing as much as it did.

Buttercups, Queen Anne's Lace, Golden Rod, Wild Asters —his grandmother would pick a handful but not many—just enough to work her magic. When they returned to his grandparents' house and his father and mother and grandfather would fall asleep in the living room and claim they were exhausted from the sunlight and fresh air, David would stand with his grandmother at the kitchen table. Between sheets of waxed paper, on top of an old Irish linen tea towel she kept aside for her pressings, she would iron each stem and its petals until they were as thin as the wax paper.

When each lock of growth was as waxed as she could make it, she would take him upstairs to the spare room where three bookcases full of fat, decorated spines of books of knowledge and Victorian novels were carefully arrayed in their ranks. She would open each book, reminding David that books had two purposes in life: one, to be read and remembered for what they said; the second to be keepers of our imaginations and memories we'd otherwise lose to time so that even when the world took away what was beautiful and helpless, there would be something between the pages to remember it by—a blossom that would mark a unique day, and time, and place.

She showed David wild roses she had pressed when she was a girl. Their petals were still yellow and white, some even retaining their pink. She showed him violets that a schoolboy had given her before he enlisted under age and never returned from overseas. She held a red rose that his grandfather had given her on the night they became engaged—it had grown in his parents' garden. And there was a sprig of lily of the valley from her bridal bouquet. Life could be measured in flowers if one refused to let them turn to dust.

Time, she said, stands still in a book. When a person reaches the end of a book, the future begins. He questioned how an ending could be a beginning, and as she laid a flowering of Queen Anne's Lace that they had brought home with them from that afternoon, she closed the cover and told him he would have to wait for the answer.

Some memories never leave a person. They become part of what one carries with them for all eternity. Maybe everyone has a soul, maybe not. But memories? Yes. The images from an event, the names of people or things, the smell of places, the taste of foods, or the texture of a piece of cloth stay with a person an entire lifetime. They become the fabric of memories. In David's case, at least as he told me during our long talks, the wildflowers of Ontario formed the omphalos of his mind. They grew out of the crevices and dry patches in his life, not literally, but inspirationally. When they died each autumn, he would look forward to them even if he was not aware that he was doing so. When they came back each spring, they assured him that life was consistent, at least in terms of wildflowers. They had been waiting in the ground for their moment to rise, and breathe the air, and be alive.

In Place

WE DON'T HAVE a lot of land. It is just enough to say we do farming when we are busy doing other things with our time. Our farm is a field and a hill. That's all. The least interesting thing about the field behind our house is its flatness before it rises to become the hill. The top of the hill has a row of white pines along the crest, but when people come to our house and look out our back door, they look beyond the field because it gets in the way. It blocks the view. When our summer crop of romaine lettuce is gone, I go over the field with a hand-held tiller that turns over the soil and leaves corduroy furrows that will fill up with snow by the end of November. I think the rows, leading away from our house toward the hill create a nice image but no one else thinks so. The field is boring. It looks too tidy with everything in place. Green in the summer, white in the winter, and that's all.

I hadn't noticed a gradual hollow growing in the northwest corner of our field. It must have been growing for several years because this year it was large and deep enough to be filled with October rain, and by early November when the cold set in, it had frozen into a small pond. I pictured myself going for a skate on it. Then I procrastinated. My skates needed sharpening. I had to drive my kids to various practices and appointments. My wife was busy with her cyber commute. I kept watching the pond. I wanted it to last, but when we hit a warm spell, it melted and disappeared.

Then, a day ago, we had rain—cold, hard rain, the kind of rain that makes life miserable, hard to drive in, and leaves a damp, raw feeling in every corner of the house no matter how hard the wood stove works or the space-heaters hum like little forges in the corners of the bedrooms. When I woke this morning and stood leaning on the kitchen countertop for my ritual black coffee in the quiet of first light before anyone in the house is awake, I glanced out the window and that's when I saw them—about twenty or more small, brown islands, creating a geography of archipelagos in our reborn pond. They were squat, short-necked, and brown as the tops of the field's furrows, and when they turned their heads from side to side, I could see the outline of their beaks. Some were turning their heads back and forth, looking at each other as if someone in their ranks had an answer or understood their predicament. They were squawking and making a terrible sound. I could hear it through the closed kitchen window. One or two flapped their wings but not a single one was lifting off. I got dressed and went out to investigate.

As I approached the pond—I've been calling it a pond but it isn't more than a foot or two deep in the lowest part of the hollow—I could see they were a flock of mallards, females, mostly, with flecks of royal blue among their mottled feathers. They must have been flying south late in the season and late at night and, looking down exhausted, seen what they thought was a watery resting place. I imagined them touching down with a splash as their bodies parted the surface and they came to a gliding stop. I could picture them in the dark, grateful to have landed like passengers after a turbulent flight, floating on the pond in the dark, tucking their heads under their wings, sitting motionless on the surface with their legs dangling beneath them.

Then the temperature dropped.

They likely didn't realize how cold it was. Water can trick warm-blooded creatures into thinking the air is warmer above them than what's beneath them. And there they were, frozen in place.

They studied me with suspicion, or what I took to be mistrust. After all, it was the season for duck hunting. They must have flown through at least one barrage of shot-gun blasts before arriving at our farm. I could have been there with a shotgun of my own and made easy pickings of them.

They saw me and couldn't do anything about it. They couldn't go anywhere. I could have been some sadist and just let them sit there and die of hunger or cold or, perhaps, snap their necks with my bare hands. But they weren't just suspicious. I could feel their fear.

They were studying me. As I moved closer to them, sliding forward slowly on the ice so I wouldn't fall, they quacked and honked disconsolately until the off-key sounds melded into a dirge or the discordant sound of a traffic jam in the city. Ducks quack when they are merely talking among themselves. Quacking to a duck is like conversation over dinner for us. They honk if they are troubled or terrified. I stared at them. They turned their heads in profile to me.

I had no idea what I was supposed to do other than get them out of the ice. When I drew close to the nearest one, it lengthened its neck and snapped at me with its beak. The duck was going to go down fighting if I was trouble. If I got too close with a chopper or an axe, I thought, I might injure one or worse. I'd have a duck on my conscience.

I have a soft spot in my heart for wild birds. To me, they represent the epitome of freedom. When geese pass over our farmhouse, honking in their southward V in autumn or vectoring north to show us one of the first signs of spring, I salute them as I would an aviator making a low pass. I respect them. I respect their beauty and their ability to fly.

On my way to and from the hospital and my work years ago, I'd pass a marsh and there was a heron who stood inscrutably among the shallows of the reeds where the water melted into the muddy shore. He never moved. He projected a powerful sense of permanence and solidity, though that was just me reading into him what I wanted from my own life at that point. I looked for him each day. He was a talisman. I needed him to be there because his presence expressed a steady patience I found reassuring. When I saw him, I'd say to myself: "Hello, Mr. Heron. Having a good day?" Stupid, but I needed to say that.

Nothing bothered him. Even when I slowed the car on the gravel shoulder, he simply stared at me. He wasn't afraid of anything. I was at a point in my life when I was afraid. Terrified, in fact. My wife was in hospital. It was touch and go. Our youngest had come too early. The doctors said my wife might need a liver transplant. They pack travelling organs in ice to convey them from the donor to the recipient. I pictured the dreadful panic of a hasty goodbye as a helicopter landed on the hospital roof and they'd be rushing my wife into surgery. Would it be the last time I held her hand? Day after day I had to wait. I had to stand up to my knees in my own fears and be patient.

There wasn't much that gave me hope as I drove those back roads. I wondered if my eldest two were going to lose their mother. Sometimes, when my eyes were full of tears and I couldn't drive any more, I'd pull over and just sit there beside Mr. Heron and we'd stare at each other. He didn't have any answers, but he was there and that was reassuring. A person looks for things like herons in a marsh when there isn't much to hold on to.

Then a cold snap came early in October and I couldn't see the heron's head, the long, thin, yellow beak, and eclipse-like eyes above the reeds even as they turned pale brown and their catkins broke and the wind carried away their cotton. And by the time the snows fell that year, hard, heavy snow, the kind that buries everything and lays a silence on the landscape and a metallic smelling crispness fills the air, I was certain the heron had simply caught wind of the changing season and given up his personal marsh and flown south. My wife's situation improved, though her recovery was invisible. She got better. Livers grow back even if it takes time. I felt as if everything had taken a turn for the better. But when a January thaw broke the surface of the marsh, I saw the heron. His body had floated out past the reeds and was drifting wherever the wind pushed him on the water.

So this morning, when I looked at the mallards, my heart sank because I knew I had to face up to my fears and if need be do battle with something beyond my control. Those ducks needed me. They weren't going to starve to death or die trying to free themselves from the grasp of ice. I had to liberate them from certain death.

I went back to the house. My wife had gotten up and watched me heading off from the shed with our ice chopper in one hand and a broken, pointy hockey stick in the other. She called and asked if I was going to drive the kids to school. I nodded but I don't think she saw it. She could see the ducks. She knew what I was going to do, and shouted: "Be careful!" As I stood at the lip of the pond, surveying the situation and formulating my strategy, I heard the car start and the voices of my kids at the side of the house.

Then I stepped onto the ice. That was my D-Day moment. I felt as if I was on the road to victory but it would be a hard slog until the last duck was free. As I drew near the birds, the flock set up that cacophony of terrible sounds. They cried as if they thought I was coming to murder them, not just stand by and stare at them as I had a few minutes earlier. The awful sound made me feel as if they thought they were going to die of fear before I could set them free. I wanted to tell them not to be afraid, that all they need fear is fear itself. The dreadful song of mortality in their throats was a prayer of the helpless looking for answers.

The first one I approached simply stared at me. It wanted to offer defiance. It reminded me of Edith Piaf singing "*Non, je ne regrette rien*." I started humming that tune softly under my breath, hoping that would quiet the flock, but they were inconsolable.

So, I began chopping.

The ice cracked but the first duck held fast. Then I began jumping up and down and the fissure I'd created opened. The duck flapped its wings and tried to fly, but its foot was held fast behind it and I was afraid it would break its leg or, worse, leave it behind like a captured starfish that doesn't want to die in a child's hand as a seaside prize.

I reached out to the bird, hoping to grab it by the body

and gently ease the leg free, but the ice snapped beneath me, and I fell through with a splash. The bird flew up into the air, its wings beating against the emptiness and fighting to be clear of what had held it in place. The other birds saw what had happened and began to flap their wings madly, sending a veil of small feathers in a cloud around them that were caught on the wind and carried upwards. "Free me now!" each one was saying. "Me first!" They saw the possibility of freedom and they wanted it.

The freed bird circled and then struck me from behind as I attempted to step back onto the ice. Water that had gone down my boot top shocked me with a soaker. I hadn't realized ducks defend each other.

Geese, yes. But ducks?

They cared for one another. Maybe each one had a unique personality. Maybe they had names and told each other jokes.

"How many ducks does it take to get stuck in a pond?"

"I dunno. How many?"

"First you gotta get them in a row and count them. Quack. Quack."

I began chopping with the scraper. I realized I wouldn't be skating any time soon, that when the pond refroze the floats of ice would leave a jagged surface. But I just wanted to get them and me out of the water and wanted more than anything to tell them that I cared for them, too, that my whole purpose for being there and getting soaked and cold first thing in the morning was their freedom.

I fell forward and my elbows snapped off another piece of ice, and the more I fought to get out of the frigid pond, the more I broke the ice. The one free bird kept attacking the back of my toque. Maybe I should have brought along some bird seed and scattered it on the ice as a peace offering before trying to do my work, but that, too, would have been meaningless.

I raised the hockey stick above my head and the attack duck got the message and flew to the far edge of the hollow. Then, I set the stick on the ice to distribute my weight and was able to stand up again. I chopped and chopped and fell in several more times until all the birds were free. They gathered with the first freed bird and waited on the far side of the pond until the last among them was clear of the ice.

They watched me from their huddle. I knew they were cold and hungry. So was I. "Are you satisfied now?" I shouted at them.

They flapped their wings ferociously and the flock lifted off into the sky.

I watched as they arranged themselves into an ordered flight. Some of them must have been older and weaker for they took positions inside the group. The stronger ones took up the front of the flight.

As I watched them, my heart sank.

They would head south. Hunters would be waiting for them. The unlucky ones would draw a bead for a direct hit or catch a spray of grapeshot biting them from the earth below or fail to rejoin the flock because they were too sick or exhausted to go on and would not live to find the rest they sought.

A duck's life is about labouring to survive—fighting the odds, struggling with the world and what the world does to them, randomly, like a sudden phone call from the hospital or a north wind across a furrowed field dusted in a light snow that appeared safe in the darkness and, yet, tricked them, deceived them with its shallow resting place, its mask of safety. To live is to live by instinct, and maybe luck, or grace, or what cannot be understood or explained and only endured. A duck's life. And a heron's, too.

For the next month, maybe longer, they would press on through the sky, fighting the winds and weather, beating their wings against the invisible force that releases them from the earth, and leaves them to nature and their determination to reach a destination in a warm place—a marsh where the trees might be draped in exotic southern moss or a salt pond where they shelter in the reeds, wary of alligators, ready to send up an alarm to the others in the flock, one eye always open and on watch for a fox or a coyote, as they wait out the winter rains falling on their backs, their heads tucked under their wings when they feel that sliver of fragile certainty as they rest. And if they dream, and who's to say they don't, would they remember the night they came to rest in a field and could not escape the terrors of a human with weapons in his hands when they were trapped in a nightmare from which they woke in the nick of time?

Restoration

THE FIRST TIME I saw Louise she was pedalling her wheelchair backwards down the long hallway in the care home. She was wearing only a nightie that she had drawn up to her arm pits, and I paused to look at her because her naked body was an encyclopaedia of skin ailments. I watched as the orderlies pushed her back to her room, much against her wishes. As the night doctor—a privilege for which the patients were charged an extra fee in the pay-as-you-go care home—I had access to her chart. She was suffering from everything from heart ailments to cirrhosis of the liver, but what was killing her slowly was time. She was one hundred and five.

No one wants to live forever, but in Louise's case she was running out of places to live. The care home only kept patients for three months. After that? Louise had no relatives. She was alone with only time to keep her company. It was anyone's guess what would become of her. I asked that she be brought down to the small office I had been given—a refitted supply cupboard—and I sat and stared at her.

I knew she couldn't hear me. The chart said she had been deaf for over twenty years. She had once worn glasses, but a previous doctor indicated that the spectacles were useless now. But she knew I was there. She knew I was trying to communicate with her. As I spoke I saw something in her eyes. She was still in there in her failing body, and as long as a patient is fighting to stay alive, as long as they tell me that they are feeling alive in whatever form that may be, I feel obligated to try and reach them. And though I was a shadowy blur I could see she was studying me with her brown eyes.

As a young man, I had furnished my apartment by finding pieces of furniture people had kicked to the curb—half a dining room table I bolted to the kitchen wall, a chair frame that required regluing, a brass bedstead that merely needed some polish. I would spend my free nights putting the chairs, tables, and other artefacts of other times and other lives back together again. Many had fine wood beneath their layers of abuse. Others, it turned out, were museum pieces waiting to be reborn. I sat studying Louise. It may have been ghoulish or wrong, but I decided to risk malpractice to restore her.

First, I began by treating her skin ailments. A person has to live inside their skin, even if they are ready to cast it off. The body is a house for the soul, but the soul, I am certain, lives on even when the body can no longer contain it. Whether our spirits seek out the bardo or the proverbial tunnel of light to the far reaches of the universe, I know there is something in us that builds up a lifetime of knowledge and experience and will not resign itself to oblivion.

A simple sugar test of her blood with a diabetic meter told me she was Type 2 and highly treatable. I ordered an oral insulin though I did not record it on her chart as I should have done. The presiding day physician would not have permitted it. I could tell from his notes that he was an adherent to the length-of-life principle, and that any means of extending or, perhaps renewing, life was not to be tolerated.

After several days of medicine, anti-oxidants and diabetic medication, Louise's eyesight returned. She could see me, though not very well. I found an old pair of glasses an elderly aunt had left behind, and they worked well enough for our late night meetings. I didn't feel I was cheating Louise of sleep. She had stopped sleeping entirely and had spent most of her nights hollering for help. The nurses ignored her pleas. She was a nuisance, they said.

Each night I gave her protein supplements on top of what she was receiving from her meals which she never ate because she had no way of knowing the food was in front of her. The home was short staffed, and Louise was gradually being starved to death. Maybe the daily attendants thought they were doing her a favour.

I brought in an old pair of hearing aids an uncle had left me—why he would will me his ear pieces was beyond me until I needed them for Louise. I discovered that Louise's ear canals were blocked by excessive wax build up, and that she had been suffering from a sinus infection at the point where her nasal passage joined the ears. After a course of antibiotics and some ear drops to loosen the wax, she began to hear me.

"I thought you were dead inside yourself," I told her one night in my closet office.

She nodded and smiled, and then, as if something was speaking through her, she began to sing. I might have expected a hymn if someone had told me that the first intelligent sound from her lips would be a musical number, but what came out was an old Rudy Vallee song, "I've Found Myself

Again." Then she added, as if an afterthought when she finished: "Bing Crosby also recorded it." Louise was returning to the land of the living.

I argued with the home's supervisor over Louise's impending release.

"You can't just turn her out. Look at the progress she is making. We are witnessing a medical phenomenon." I didn't want to use the word miracle. The medical profession does not believe in miracles. They are unscientific.

I back-and-forthed with the administrator for over an hour. The administrator said that they needed Louise's bed for another patient.

"Is the other patient dying?" The administrator wouldn't tell me.

But I won. I would pay for Louise's additional care out of my salary—something I couldn't afford—and Louise would continue to improve, though I could not record my treatments of her various conditions. We met each night in my broom-closet office and gradually she unfolded her life story to me.

She had been beautiful once, she said, and wanted more than anything to be beautiful again. "Ah," she said, sighing, "beauty belongs only to the young."

"But can't you see I am making you young?" I held up a hand mirror I had borrowed from a younger patient.

"That's not me."

"It is you. You are making a comeback. You are undoing the ravages of time."

"Time kills everyone," she said. "It kills the body, but it also kills the soul by poisoning all hope."

"Do you still have hope?" I asked. "Look. Look the mirror. You are growing younger by the minute, and minute by minute hope is returning to you. You told me that years ago you had been a dancer in a speak-easy. A flapper. I'm not sure there's much call for that now, but you are making tremendous progress. I want to see you dance again."

She laughed at me. I have never been one to tell an elderly person there is no hope. My father had insisted he was going to die on Good Friday at precisely eleven a.m. I had told him he would not, and what had made him so sure?

He replied that he had been visited by a dark angel and the angel had called his time and day of death exactly a week before. When I left him in his hospital room late on Holy Thursday evening, alone in his private Gethsemane, he told me that I didn't care. Those were his last words to me. He had fixed the time and day in his mind and was determined to fulfill his agreement with a shadow. But I would not surrender hope for Louise and I told her so.

Her cheeks had filled in again and her colour was healthy. I had replaced her cracked dentures with teeth made by a dentist friend of mine who cautioned that I needed to be careful, that the whole thing could backfire on me, that I could ruin my career. He reminded me of the "do-no-harm" oath I had taken, but I had assured him that finding life beneath the layers of time and pain inflicted on a person could only be a good thing. I was walking a very thin ethical line.

The vitamins were making her hair come in sable at the roots, just as it had been, she said, when she was a young woman in love. The snow that had been in her hair fell softly outside the window of the home, covering the lawn and trees while Louise's hair grew long enough to cut off the white and give her a Twenties bob cut. By the end of the winter, Louise was ready to be released from the home.

On the day of her release, I was summoned to the home. The doctors, especially the gerontologists, could not understand how the transformation had taken place. This was not right, they insisted. Louise is one hundred and six going on one hundred and seven. She should have died by then. And because I needed my job, I dared not wheel anyone else from their rooms in the dead of the night to restore the human being that was still alive inside a broken body.

In retrospect, I am not sure I could do what I had done for her for anyone else. It wasn't just that Louise had a strong heart, a heart that had kept her alive when everything else about her gave the appearance of death—the lovers who had abandoned her, the hungry years of the Great Depression, the hard labour of unskilled work when she cleaned office buildings at night until she was ninety and bent over from pushing a broom. What had been the key to Louise was that she was alive, vital and determined to fight her way out of her incarcerating body in search of the life she was certain she still possessed.

I wheeled her into the sunroom as my shift began on her last night in the home. The hallways were dark. The patients were sleeping. Down the hall we could hear someone's television set and the strains of Irish dance music echoing in the darkness while the viewer slept.

"Please let me come and live with you," Louise said, begging. I had thought long and hard about the possibility that she might want to attach herself to me for longer than the course of my treatment, but at that point I grew afraid. I became a doctor rather than a healer. I could not bring myself to form any sort of personal relationship with her. It would have been the final wrong in a litany of broken boundaries.

She now had the appearance of a young woman of thirty.

It might have been good to extend our relationship. She had become beautiful again, but what she had told me during our long nights of treatment made me fear her. She knew so much more of the world than I did. She carried the weight of accumulated experience that I would have to live a lifetime to acquire. Some would call it the age gap. I call it the need to learn of life on my own terms.

I told her, no.

She would have to make her own way in the world, just as she had done before. And having done it before she would know the way better now. I wheeled her out of my tiny office and closed the door. She began to weep and tried to open it, then banged with her fists on the barrier that stood between us.

Then she fell silent, and I heard her say: "This door is Time. You once opened it for me and now you have closed it. What do I have to live for now?" That was the last thing she said to me.

I had no answer.

I fear death.

I fear seeing it in others and I fear seeing myself in them.

I thought it was empathy that made me want to reach out to her and return what had been taken from her. Then I explained it to myself as a man of science and medicine—that I *was* doing no harm. And yet I had harmed her in a way I could not have harmed someone my own age. I had no endgame for what I had done. Leaving a person without the mercy of time is, perhaps, the worst harm one can do.

I could hear her sobs as she walked down the hallway to the front door where a taxi was waiting for her. And as she wept, I imagined the years flooding back into her face, her eyes, and her trembling lips, until they filled her body once again, and I was helpless to stop the flood of silence.

Empty

JOSHUA CAME UP to me at the shiva with a glass of whisky in his hand, and in a reserved toast touched his dram to mine. The shiva for Harriet had been more like an Irish wake, and Joshua was deeply troubled by several things that afternoon—his mother's death, the fact that he had not been there in the end of hear the prayers said upon her dying, or to stand at the graveside where she had been laid to rest. Joshua had not been able to make a connecting flight and having sat in one departure lounge after another as he hopped from destination to destination of small civic airports and never got nearer to home with each snakes and ladder move. He felt bitter. He was angry my mother was alive when his wasn't. It was the grief or the drink talking. Probably both.

Death is a shared occasion, but I felt as if I was intruding. As the son of an Irish immigrant, I had identified with Joshua's mother, Harriet, who had grown up in Dublin. She told me of the night in 1942 when the German bombers, whether by accident, or on purpose, or on the orders of de Valera who no one trusted except the priests, had levelled the Jewish district of the city. Her father and uncle were sitting shiva at the time for a local mohel who had passed from a lung infection. They never knew what hit them. The house of mourners had been blown apart, and Harriet's connection to the language of her ancestors was severed in that moment. Her mother, an English woman, had converted to Judaism to marry Harriet's father. In the wake of that bloody night in 1942 when the Germans mistook Dublin, two hundred miles away, for Bristol, and only bombed the Irish city's Jewish district, Harriet's mother—possibly out of fear and possibly because she felt alone in a land of strangers, did not even whisper the traditions Harriet should have learned.

When Harriet came to Canada, she studied her faith from the beginning. She had said it was a rebirth. A voice, she said, awoke inside her. Then, having recovered what she felt was rightfully hers, Harriet married an Irishman, an older friend of mine who had been an altar boy. The memorial for Harriet was both a shiva and an Irish wake.

I stumbled in my mind to give Joshua an answer. I'd been into the drink for over an hour. I tried to explain to Joshua that connections are never as permanent as we would wish them and as that came out it sounded awful to me; then I addressed whether the connection of faith or culture or life are things we lose forever, that maybe we carry them with us in our hearts. I sounded like an ass-end priest. Joshua repeated the question. He still wanted to know why my mother lived and his was dead. I told him I didn't have an answer, but that I loved my mother, wanted to hold on to her, and treasured the time we had already spent together. I remembered sitting on her knee as a small child and learning the Lord's Prayer by heart.

"What did she teach you?" I asked.

"What sort of fucked up question is that?"

"Did she pass on the traditions to you? Did you go to Hebrew school or at least celebrate Passover or Shabbat?"

He glared at me. I thought he was either going to punch me or throw his drink in my face. That would have been an appropriate response to my bluntness, at least from his Irish heritage. "Yes. She did all those things."

The Irish music from a tenor in the next room, accompanied by a fiddle and a tin flute, suddenly fell silent. I heard a deep voice intoning something ancient, something profound and sad. Joshua turned away from me to listen. I leaned against the dining room table and stared into my glass. I saw my reflection in the water of life.

When the Kaddish ceased, the music resumed, but it was joined by a clarinet and a piano, and the tenor broke into a song that was punctuated by shouts of joy.

Joshua turned to me. "So, you haven't answered my question."

"I can't. I'm sorry. There is no explanation for either life or death. There is only the time we have in this world to do the things that make being in this world tolerable for ourselves and for others."

"I've spent ten years of my life wandering," he said. The tears were welling in his eyes. "I'm going to have to keep looking. I just don't know what the fuck to do."

"Well, if there's the half of it as my family says, it is that we are wanderers. There's the old belief that the Irish are the lost tribe of Israel. Both the Irish and the Jews—we are peoples who have been scattered by time and history and are constantly searching for something we can't name until we fall down, drunk or exhausted, or broken-hearted by God. We live. We suffer. We rise from our sufferings and go in search of more because that's where life drives us. Not curiosity, just life. We wander. We all wander, I guess. The only way to find something is to look for it, and if it isn't out there somewhere, it might be right under our noses. That's the best I can do for an answer."

"Empty," he said. Just that one word "empty." He patted my shoulder and moved deeper into the gathering.

I heard Joshua had gone to the Far East. I saw a photograph on his Facebook page. He was standing on a mountain top, looking into the horizon and wondering where it would take him or whether there was an answer to his questions at the end of it. His post was captioned simply, "I don't know, but it has to be there."

Star of Wonder

CLARITY HAD BEEN a long time returning. First the accident and the head injury, then the nervous breakdown. His employer had been tolerant of the accident. That hadn't been Ern's fault. The boss was far less sympathetic about the breakdown. The language, the awful verbal assaults on his co-workers and their loud music at the Christmas party, and then the fit of weeping, had been the last straw. Besides, Ern had been around a long time. Once upon a time, longevity in a job would have meant something; but now it was a case of an old guy not being able to keep up with the intuitive skills of the office. He never knew what button to push except the one that upset everyone.

Ern and his wife, Erma, sold their home in the spring and moved into a midtown condo "to be close to things," as Erma put it. The condo had large windows and good light. Erma thought it would help bring Ern back from the inner death he told her he was experiencing in the wake of his "fall from heaven." Just when he looked like he was making progress, though, he had bad moments. Ern brought a dinner party to silence a week before when he had insisted, over dessert and his fifth glass of wine, the angel choir that appeared to the shepherds when Jesus was born were the demonic rebel angels on their way down to the ground when Satan fell. "I mean, do angels talk to us the rest of the time? Who else would wreak such havoc through overheated stores, nauseating music everywhere, and chintzy glass balls on trees?"

Ern should have been hung over the next morning when he woke early and stood at the balcony door, but a change had come to him in the night. He felt different. He felt organized inside his head. The rooftops of the city skyline were steaming. The night had been bitter cold, but the clouds had passed, and the dawn was an unusual purple. For the first time in years, he could see without his glasses. He could read the license plates of cars in the street below. The fog had left his mind. He felt good about himself. He felt he had the strength to face the world again. He had clarity. The clarity should have stayed with him, but by Christmas day it had gone somewhere else.

Their eldest daughter, Ella, who still lived in the city, came for the big day, and brought her two boys with her. They were loud and cranky and he wanted to tell them they were brats but thought better about calling them names in front of their mother. She was doing her best. Her mothering just wasn't good enough. Ern figured it was the lack of a father figure in their lives, someone like his own father who would lay down the law and set things straight. Ella's husband had walked out on his family a year ago, at Christmas time, and Ella had fled to her parents for support. Ern wanted to think of the boys as urchin, but he felt too sorry for the pair to let his mind wander into speculation about what would become of them. "Just love them and be there for them, Dad," Ella had pleaded. Ern was tired of being the father figure. The boys needed their own old man, not an old man who'd done his time and been faithful to his wife and his fatherly duties.

Neither of the boys was happy with what Santa had brought them. They kept calling their grandfather Ern Poo because he refused to be called Grandpa, or Bumpa, or Boo-boo, and the word Poo irritated the hell out of him. The boys knew this. "Poo, Poo," they said over and over again whenever he tried to sit down and enjoy a drink. Christmas was the one day of the year Erma let Ern enjoy a succession of gin and tonics. The more he tried to enjoy himself, the more the blurriness returned to his brain, and the more the boys taunted him.

Ern's old, limping dog was the last vestige of a time when his family had been happy. Caper was the one creature he could trust in the chaos inside his head to know which way to turn on their walks through the streets of apartment towers. The boys were louder than a catastrophe of steel. Erma and Ella argued over the thickness of the gravy and the amount of salt in the mashed potatoes. The sunset was hanging over a long day that was becoming longer. Ern's head began to bang from the inside. Caper needed to go out for a crap.

Ern got up the strength to get dressed in his overcoat and scarf and boots and took the dog down in the elevator. A woman on the second floor—he had run-ins with her in the past because she let her Yorkie loose and his dog, a mongrel, disliked all other dogs, especially small ones—was waiting for them at the elevator door, and in a moment of chaos, through the haze of the gin Ern had consumed, he was startled to find he wasn't at the ground floor and his dog was lunging at the small, white thing. He pulled his dog back into the elevator just before there was any bloodshed, but it shook Ern. He stared at his dog and the dog looked up at him, sheepish, as if to say: "Well, I like what I like."

In the snow-covered rose garden, his dog sniffed about in the darkness. Ern felt the cold sinking down the back of his neck. He wanted to do up his coat but was cautious another dog might suddenly appear, and he would lose control of the situation and shriek at the owner and possibly take a swing at the person. He didn't want that. He wanted peace on earth, as the motto of the day suggested. The dog squatted and turned and looked relieved before going back to her sniffing.

In the upper level of the condo garden, there were readers' benches, a nice place on a summer day and a lonely place on a winter night. The dog pulled Ern over the edge of the shovelled walk. He was standing past the top of his boots in the piled white shovelling. The dog tugged again, and Ern lost his balance and fell over into a patch of unbroken snow.

He wanted to scream when his head hit the ground but who would hear him? He lay there, staring up at the stars, uncertain if they were astral or cerebral. Caper stood above his face, licked it, and then sat down. If this was how defeat felt, Ern thought, it was about falling, not once or even twice, but over and over again. He had become a fall artist in so many ways. Falling was the one thing he had to show for the effort he had put into his life. The kids were right. He was a piece of Poo.

He looked up. In a subsidized housing apartment tower behind his condo, someone had hung a banner of electric lights that flashed Merry Christmas from a balcony. He hated that kind of junk. Merry, he remembered, meant sexual abandon. It was a word that meant walking out on one's family, and at Christmas. He'd said to Ella's husband when they met, by accident, downtown one morning: "I bet you're having a merry time." And the guy had pushed him over, landing Ern on his backside. It was a shame humans weren't angels. When it came to the complexities of sex and commitment, the urges of the jolly trouser elf were what made humans awful. All an angel had to do for sex was just think about it with another angel. Nice and clean. No one gets hurt. No kids needing a father on Christmas. It would be nice to be an angel.

He waved his arms and his legs in the snow. So, this is what fallen angels feel like, he thought. And then he saw it. He saw how far he had fallen, and what was still there, shining through the gathering storm clouds of his future—a light in the stairwell of the subsidized building, a light that was brighter than all the others. It blinded him, but even when he closed his eyes he could see it. It had come to rest over the top floor of the tower and it shone as if it wanted to mark a special place.

When he stood up and the dog pulled on the leash, he paused, looked down at the angel his body had made where he fell. The outline of his body, and perhaps his soul, was small and needed a halo. He staggered to the head-end of the imprint and began to weep as he bent and drew a halo over its head with his gloved index finger. His shoulders heaved up and down and the dog looked at him, then at the star in the tower, and moved closer to nuzzle against his left leg. And as Ern sank to one knee to pat the dog or to genuflect to the star—he wasn't sure which—he knew he was drunk, but he was certain the dog was trying to say: "Look! What a clear night it has become."

Cadenza

WHEN WE WERE kids, my brother and I would lie in our bunk beds at night long after we were told lights out by our parents. Because I was older, I got the upper bunk. My brother's great fear was that I would grow too fast, as I did, and that upper bed would collapse on the lower, crushing him. He always said he hated being in my shadow. I was good at school and sports and he wasn't. He was always screwing up in small ways. I got away with far too much. When I took piano lessons—Tony had no patience for music—he asked me why I was making up part of the piece I was supposed to be learning.

"That's the cadenza," I said. "It's the stuff you make up when no one tells you what to do."

"Like us," he said.

"I don't follow."

"Well, you're always telling me what to do even when you don't know what you're doing. I know when you make stuff up. I just go along with it. You're the big brother. Someday, I'm going to get to call the shots. I'm going to be the one to make stuff up."

He followed me everywhere, even when I didn't want him to.

On one of my dates when I was sixteen, as I was kissing a girl named Arrieta who was known for her kissing and for loving to be fondled, my brother showed up in our basement where Arrieta and I were busy on the old couch and asked what I was doing. I told him to get lost. He stood there and stared. He knew full-well what I was doing. He was being a pest.

Later, I told him that when he got to be my age, I was going to spoil a night of his, and he replied: "Go ahead. Someday, I will not only follow you around, I will beat you to something important."

We grew older. We went our separate ways. We tried to stay in touch, but it was hard. We had family obligations, work responsibilities. And then, a month ago, I got a call saying Tony had passed. Just like that. Passed. I hung up the phone and sat on the edge of the bed in stunned silence. It was the middle of the night. I should have been up late reading with a flashlight beneath the blankets like my brother and I used to do when we shared a room and comic books, but instead I was lying in the dark beside my wife. She propped herself on one elbow and asked what the call was about.

"Tony's gone," I said. She reached to turn on the light. I told her not to. "There's nothing to do right now. Go back to sleep. Please, go back to sleep."

We used to have plaid blankets on our bunk beds and cowboy sheets. Those were the fads for boys when we were young. There was one cowboy who always seemed out of place from the other figures in the pattern who were breaking bucking broncos or shooting up the streets of a frontier town. The lonesome cowboy was riding off into the sunset, his head down. One night we talked about our sheets.

"I bet I know where he's going," Tony told me.

"Okay. Where? I think he's pony express taking the slow route."

"Not going to tell you," he said as he turned over and switched off the wall-mounted light beside his bunk. "But he's going to get there ahead of anyone else and they're going to make him the sheriff. Anyone after him will be the odd hombre in town when that happens."

When the funeral finally concluded, and Tony was lowered into the ground, his wife sobbing, his children clinging to her sleeve, it was late in the afternoon. The February sun was setting between the headstones. I stared at the orange glow off to the west and could have sworn I saw that lonesome cowboy again, his head bent, his horse exhausted, putting one hoof ahead of the other because there was some place he was destined to be even if he took the slow way to get there first.

A Month of Good Luck

MRS. MULVEENY SUBSCRIBED to the old tradition that a person would have a month of good luck for every piece of Christmas cake consumed outside the home between Christmas and New Year's. One home, one piece, one month was the formula for fine fortune.

She had experienced a hard year. The familiar faces of her St. Vincent de Paul group at the church had vanished one by one. She had tried her best to attend their funerals, but she had difficulty getting about to houses, nursing homes, and elder care facilities in the suburbs where her friends had been taken to live out their last days. The reality was that Mrs. Mulveeny was growing forgetful, and with each passing day's difficulties came a new illusion that her departed friends had not, in fact, died.

As had been her custom, she began her circuit of friends on Boxing Day. She put on her black Persian lamb coat and the feathered black hat that matched and, leaning on her cane for steadiness, made her way up the street. Mrs. Calder would be her first stop.

She mounted the steps of the veranda, knocked on the door, lifting the heavy bronze knocker and letting it fall—it was her trademark knock for Mrs. Calder—and stood in the chill silence. No one came to the door. She raised herself on her toes to see in through the panes of bevelled glass in the door, but no one was home. She turned and left, and made herself a cup of tea when she got in.

Life was not getting any easier. On the twenty-seventh, Mrs. Mulveeny followed the same routine, and arrived at Mrs. Harrington's house only to find a young woman answering the door with a six-month-old baby and trailing a nursing blanket in her arms.

"I'm afraid Mrs. Harrington no longer lives here. She passed on last April and we purchased the house in July. I'm sorry if you didn't know. Were you a friend of Mrs. Harrington's?"

Mrs. Mulveeny explained that she and Mrs. Harrington had been part of the St. Vincent de Paul Society at St. Agatha's, and that, yes, indeed, it was very sad. She offered the young woman an apology for troubling her and tried to explain the Christmas cake tradition that she and her friends had kept for the past forty years ... since they had all moved to the parish with young children in their arms.

"Yuck. Christmas cake," the young mother replied. "I'm sorry, I'd ask you in, but we don't have any."

As the young woman closed the door, Mrs. Mulveeny felt as if she had seen that tableau before somewhere—a mother holding a child in her arms but could not make the connection in her mind to any specific reason for the reminiscence.

The twenty-eighth was no better. Mrs. Parkington did not answer either. A neighbour called from the next veranda, perhaps concerned that Mrs. Mulveeny might be wandering again and on the icy sidewalks. "Yoo-hoo! Mrs. Parkington has gone to Florida to be with her dying sister. She will be back in February, perhaps sooner if, you know, if she is able to return." The woman offered to take a message for her, but Mrs. Mulveeny thanked her and said it would not be necessary.

On the twenty-ninth it snowed heavily, as it did on the thirtieth, and glancing out her living room window after parting the tergals, Mrs. Mulveeny decided not to go out.

Every hour, she checked on the snow. It fell unabated. It felt as if it was a white sheet that was wound around her head and eyes. She could not see past it.

The hours ticked away and chimed on the mantel clock. The new year came in quietly as she sipped the last few ounces of a bottle of Bailey's she had kept at the back of the refrigerator since her husband passed away three years before. The drink tasted slightly off. She would have to get a magnifying glass and check the label to see if there was an expiry date.

It struck her that so many things, even in the cold of winter, would not keep. She remembered the laughter, the faces. She recalled how Father Philip patted her on the back and thanked her and her St. Vincent de Paul sisters for their Christian service to the poor.

"You shall have the good fortune of a fine place in heaven for all your hard work," he had told them. Perhaps Christmas cake wasn't necessary after all.

She sat with the sound turned off on her television as the crystal ball descended in Times Square and couples with their arms around each other kissed as clouds of breath formed white shawls, white as the mantle of the Virgin, around their heads. She forgot about the Christmas cake and thought to herself: "Yes, love will go on. Love is the only thing one needs to get by on. The rest is what one makes of it."

She assured herself that luck has nothing to do with friendship and love, though one is lucky to have friendship and love, and *that* never leaves one even in moments of profound exhaustion when one is all alone and too tired to go on and not a crumb of Christmas cake anywhere. Maybe the new year would be different.

Snow fell on the house where she had raised a son and lost a son and a husband, and she dreamed of a beautiful white silence that filled the room with a whole year or more of everlasting joy.

The Smell of Spring

THEY HAD COME to a compromise and moved to the edge of a small town not far from Gary's work. Behind their house were cornfields in the summer, and drifting expanses of snow devils on winter days when the sun was almost appearing through the grey overcast. They were far away from their relatives—Michele's were in Montreal and those of his still living were down in the city, though he hadn't spoken to them in years.

Gary and his father had a falling out over a fishing rod. Family relationships never crumble along the obvious fault lines but at the hairline cracks that can be traced to older arguments. Gary's grandfather had taken him fishing and, without telling his own son that he was being passed over for the rod, had given it to his grandson. The resentment grew from there. Both Gary and his father considered the rod a kind of sceptre to the family legacy, and as a crown jewel of authority, Gary's father felt slighted that he had not been the chosen one. He asked Gary for the rod. Gary refused. In the back of Gary's mind, he had always pictured himself living away from the city, somewhere rural, perhaps on a piece of land where a decent-sized river ran through the back forty and he could cast his line and daydream, if he ever got the time.

Living on the dividing line between the country and the town was pleasant and peaceful but often troubled Michele. They were a long way from a grocery store and even farther from a hospital. She and Gary had to drive anywhere they wanted to go. To get in the spirit of the rural life, they had sold their gas conserving sedans for sport utility vehicles that ate the miles but burned holes in their wallets. But what made them want to stay where they were, despite the crop dusting that took place once a year and the ugly clouds of heaven-knows-what that would scatter the birds for several hours after the plane passed low over the stalks, was the smell of the country when the country was able to be itself, expressing the aroma of rain on wood bark, or the musk of earth on a spring morning before the farming commenced again in earnest.

Having lived the better part of their married lives in the city, the country air made them feel alive. In the summer, there was a dustiness that hung in the breeze especially late in the day or just after the rain let up, the scent of green that stayed in the grass each morning and wove through the rows of corn carrying a sweetness with it that reminded Michele of her mother who had been an avid gardener. It was the aroma of sunburnt skin and hands that had touched living things. For Gary, the falling leaves of mid-October and the foist of the first frost on them was special. It was the smell of life, and it reminded him that life is short, and in that brevity, he had to make the best of it even if it meant turning his back on a man whom he had once adored no matter how far apart they always appeared to be in distance or thought or belief.

The smell of the country in late March intrigued Gary and Michele despite their preferences for opposing seasons. Michele loved the fall. Gary marvelled when spring broke the ice in the roadside ditches and burst the twigs in their wood lot to life in a matter of a few warm hours.

Most of the farms over the rise in the road beyond the horizon of the nearest field had wood lots, and those stands of old maple would run with sap every March. After the last hard snows had fallen, when the sun would appear by day to warm the bodies of the trees and the stars would slowly pass over the treetops on clear, cold nights so that the highest branches appeared to try to pluck the points of light, the trees would bleed a sweetness into miles of plastic tubing that connected the maples as if each rooted life was part of a mass transfusion. Once the sap was running, it was collected in white butter buckets and brought to the sugar shacks where it would be boiled for hours. The aroma of the sugaring off process was the scent of the back-concessions in the spring. The steam the sugaring off produced would hang in the air and Gary would remember his grandfather's pipe smoke when they fished together at a long-lost cottage.

Gary had just come in from the deck off the kitchen where he had stood long and thoughtfully, looking up at the stars and inhaling the aroma of late March when he clutched at his left arm and collapsed on the floor. Michele heard the thud from her reading chair in the living room and came running. Hours passed while Michele frantically waited for the ambulance to arrive, for the paramedics to make the long drive to the nearest hospital, and for the doctor to be summoned to reach a verdict on Gary's condition. When she was permitted to see him, he was still motionless, his eyes closed.

Did he know she was there with him? Would he live or die? Was there brain damage from the delay in getting treatment? He had told her, just that morning, he was looking forward to seeing the apple blossoms in May. "Spring is just around the corner," he said.

Gary did not know Michele was there. He was walking out into the field behind the house with his hands in the pockets of his roll-neck sweater. The corn had not yet been seeded, though the fields were dry and solid. He thought it odd that the farmer had not gotten his usual jump on the season. He worried that the land might have been sold to a developer without his knowledge. He feared the tang of fresh lumber, the gritty stone smell of new brickwork being laid, and the mouldy pungency of earth being turned over deep down after lying undisturbed since the stumps had been pulled almost two centuries before. He walked beyond the horizon line of the field where the sky appeared to meet the earth and crested the horizon. In an orchard he had never noticed before were apple boughs draping like bridal veils that adorned the ranks of trees. As far as he could see, the orchard was bursting with life. Each tiny flower would grow, in time, to become an apple.

The boughs were rustling before him and some of the petals began to drop. Gary resented this. "Who's there?" he asked.

"Me," the voice replied, and with that his father emerged, stooped, and rising upright as he moved forward to the clear path between the rows where Gary was standing.

Gary did not know what to say. After not speaking for so long, the first thing to say would be difficult.

His father spoke first.

"We both had a rough night of it. I was sitting watching

television and I fell asleep. It wasn't much of a program. Same stuff. A detective and his crime lab looking for a murderer."

"I know what you mean."

"Well, Gary, this is May. This is what the future looks like. Everything is blooming. Everything is moving on with its purpose. The apples will be good this year. The nodes are strong."

"I didn't know you knew much about apples," Gary replied. "I always took you for a city guy who would take a week at a cottage and leave the rest for somebody else."

"True. I was. I was a selfish guy. A city guy. I never took the time to notice much about what the world did on its own. I always thought I had to make things happen. I should have had more to do with you and your grandfather. He would call me up late at night when you were asleep and tell me about the great day you had out on the lake, how many bass or perch or sharks or whatever you'd caught. I was envious, but I was where I was. And had to be. Hey, remember on Saturday mornings when you were very young, while your mother was still asleep, I'd pour some milk on your favourite breakfast cereal and we'd watch those corny westerns where the hero lands a plane in the middle of nowhere, always in the middle of nowhere, and he jumps out and punches the bad guy?"

"Yes, I remember those."

"Well, he'd always say: 'This place ain't big enough for the both of us.'"

"So, what about it?"

"Well, son, this place ain't big enough for the both of us. So, see you later."

Gary woke with a jolt. Michele, asleep beside her husband's hospital bed in a large, grey, reclining chair, heard him utter "Uh!" and opened her eyes.

"You're back," she whispered, smiling.

"I just saw my Dad. He was in an orchard with me and the trees were all in bloom. It was beautiful, but he and I—we never made our peace. I could have said something, but I didn't know what to say."

Michele was silent for a moment as she stroked Gary's forehead. "Just lie back and rest. The doctor says you'll need rehab but if you work at it and get some walking in when you're ready, you'll be strong again. As I said this morning, spring is just around the corner. We'll walk together."

Gary closed his eyes. He wanted to see the orchard, but for the moment it was too far away, and he would have to wait, perhaps for years, to taste the apples he knew were out there waiting for him and to stand among the boughs and breathe the perfume of the trees. Even with the tubes in his nostrils he was certain the smell of spring had followed him back from the orchard over the crest.

Consuelo

A MAN IN the bus station stood staring into the black screen of his dead cell phone as he shouted her name as if he had been wounded and was suffering from a great pain. He shouted it as if he was falling to his knees in the rain and begging forgiveness or pleading for a second chance.

But what caught my attention was a kid whom I couldn't see who was near the banquette behind me and who kept pacing up and down, talking in a noticeable New York-Queens accent about how there weren't any girls in this town and he was coming back to New York because he'd left all his gaming equipment in his old room and he didn't want the person on the other end of the conversation to pitch it out if he didn't return.

And as I looked around the bus station where mothers usually waited late at night with their sleeping children on the seats beside them, or college girls stared at their laptops and chewed gum while listening to their playlists through umbilical ear buds, or old women in head scarves sat nervously on the edge of their seats, clutching at their black shoulder bags because the sound of revving bus engines reminded them of being deported at gun-point when they were children, I looked up and all the women were gone.

I waited ten, fifteen minutes or more because my bus wouldn't be leaving for another hour in the middle of the night, and not a single woman appeared. There were only men, some of them old, some of them young, sitting, staring straight ahead, and empty-eyed as if they had all been struck dumb in disbelief. They didn't speak amongst themselves. I couldn't speak to them. I had nothing to say. And the kid from New York who kept asking someone on the other end of the cell phone call if they were there, repeated "Hello? Hello?" and slapped the phone in the palm of his hand several times as if it wasn't working. And the man with the dead cell phone and blackened screen who had called out for Consuelo, leaned against a pillar and wept over what, he told me, he couldn't remember about the light he had known in her eyes.

Looking Good

DAVE IS WHAT'S known as an early barber. He opens early and closes early. He had just warmed up the lather machine and was setting his scissors and cut-throats out on the clean terry-towel when the first customer arrived. He did not look up. "I'm just getting ready for you," he said.

"People are rarely ready for me," the stranger in black said. "I have come."

Dave still did not look up. He glanced in the mirror at the backwards clock—something barbers hang on their walls to measure their moments so they don't chat too long to a friend, or tell too many jokes, or go on about local events and who has been doing what and it was just ten past five. Ten past five in the morning is the hour when people slip silently from this world, some in their sleep going peaceably, some struggling and fighting to the last ounce of their strength, and some just as they are easing their feet out of bed and setting them on the floor.

The stranger came over and sat down in the chair. Dave lifted the black hood from the customer's head and exposed the bone of a bald skull. He laughed and shook his head. "Haven't left me much to work with." Dave glanced out the front window to the street and the first light was just breaking along the avenue. Then he saw the face of Death in the mirror, though not the actual face. He saw the reflection of Death and himself standing over the skull-headed figure.

"I am here for you. I am Death, the Grim Reaper."

"You don't say. Seeing as how you are here, you could probably use a haircut?" Dave said, smiling at the smile he saw in the mirror. "Even Death can't go around looking shaggy." The customer's expression did not change. "How about I make a deal with you. If I can give you a haircut, and you pay for it, you can go away and come back in a few weeks when you've got something and if I can give you a haircut each time then we'll keep things square, you and me. If you don't have anything for me to cut, then I'll be your guest."

"Sounds fair," Death said.

Dave began to snip at imaginary hairs when he noticed that, stuck in the joint of his shears, a long grey hair protruded from the screw. He'd missed it the day before when he was cleaning up. He'd been in a hurry. When he closed, he always had somewhere to go to with so little time to get there. Even today, when he closed at noon, he had promised to take his wife shopping.

Dave tapped the scissors on the back of the chair, but as he brought them down he pulled the strand from the joint and proceeded to snip. "Well, what do you know? You do have something."

Death sat up straight in the chair, surprised. He held up the lone hair and placed it in Death's hand. "There you go. See? You did need a haircut. You might be Death or the Grim Reaper, but you still got some life in you, at least enough for a haircut!"

The barber set his scissors on the towel, picked up a bottle of green liquid, and poured a handful of pine-scented *eau de cologne* in the palm of his hand. He rubbed it over Death's bald pate, and then picked up the mirror to show the dark figure the beauty of his barber arts. "All done. That'll be twelve fifty."

Death stood, fumbled with his long, dirty cloak, reached into his pocket and drew out a ten and a five.

"Keep the change," Death said to the barber. "I'll be back when I need another."

"Any time," Dave said. "Always a pleasure. I'm here and open early."

THE MIDDLE

The Muse

BOBBY SHOVED PHIL in the microwave. They'd been best buddies since they were young.

In those days, Phil hardly said a word and Bobby was a lonely boy who people claimed was "troubled." Yet no matter what passed between them, Phil trusted Bobby implicitly. He would stare at Bobby with his wide eyes. Sometimes Phil would even blink. Sometimes Phil would smile because whatever Bobby did moved Phil in ways that made Phil feel alive. In many ways, Phil was Bobby's muse, and Bobby was often astounded at what came out when Phil spoke and made Bobby think that a spirit animated every joint of his best pal.

They had gone to school together until Bobby was teased, then beaten up, then cast out of friendships by the other kids because he insisted that wherever he went Phil had to go. Phil, he insisted, was helpless, and a few of the kinder kids felt empathy for Bobby's pal, with his limp body that Bobby pushed around the school in a small, wheeled chair.

Some of the girls Bobby asked out on dates during his sophomore and senior years at high school found Phil's company amusing at first, but if Bobby began to get close to any of them Phil always had to throw in his two cents worth and ruin things. One girl asked why Bobby just didn't dump his friend. After all, Phil was starting to wear thin on the less patient girls who laughed at Phil's jokes, at first, then didn't.

When Bobby graduated from university and proposed to his sweetheart, it was Phil who told her that she could do far better than Bobby if she looked harder and wasn't so willing to settle for less. Despite what Phil said, however, Doris accepted Bobby's earnest proposal and spoke sharply to Phil. It was, after all, none of Phil's goddamned business. Bobby apologized and told Doris that Phil was more or less a brother to him, that despite the physical limitations and awkwardness, Phil was really a good soul at heart, someone who just wanted to love and be loved in ways Bobby would know and Phil could not. One night when Bobby and Doris were making love, they stopped, lay in the dark, and were certain they could hear Phil weeping.

As Bobby's marriage began to deteriorate, Phil became more of a problem. Whenever the three of them went out for dinner or a drink, Phil insisted that he practice his enunciation, and was certain he would someday master the words "bottle of beer" despite all the warnings that no amount of practice would ever overcome the impossibility of pronouncing that simple phrase. The beers, not just in bottles or cans, but jugs of draught served in increasingly larger mugs, would accumulate on their table. Even when Doris waved the waitresses off, Bobby had to down them all because he felt sorry for his pal, and the problem was not really Phil's but Bobby's. Doris would slide a glass in front of Phil, but Phil always begged off because of his delicate condition. "It goes right through me," he would explain. One day, Doris had enough. She packed her belongings and drove away.

"You still have me to talk to," Phil said, offering to console Bobby. "C'mon, Bobby. Be my muse. You inspire me and fill me with life."

But Bobby began to think Phil was the root of all evil in his life—the reason Bobby couldn't hold a job, the master of deception behind his broken relationships, the voice that simply wouldn't shut up even in the moment of silent remembrance at Bobby's father's funeral. Phil had to go, and Phil knew it. For several days he sat in his place at the kitchen table and just stared at Bobby, distrustful yet hopeful that the good old days, the days when Bobby's friends who loved Phil's jokes would gather around them to hear Phil sing and to watch him spin his head three hundred and sixty degrees.

Bobby knew that putting Phil in the microwave was going to be a messy business. After all, he told himself without moving his lips so Phil would not hear or even read his thoughts, the oven would overheat, spark, and explode, perhaps burn down the horrible basement apartment to which Bobby had resigned his life with Phil. Microwaving Phil would be his salvation.

"Talk to me, Bobby," Phil pleaded as his dearest companion shoved his limp left arm into the door after it caught during Bobby's first attempt to close it. "Please, Bobby. I can change. I can try to hold my peace. Remember when I begged you never to put me back in the box? You tossed that away. That was a fresh start. We can do another fresh start. Can't we?"

But Bobby said nothing. He wondered how long it would take, whether Phil would suffer, or if the process would burn the apartment down. He felt he could never say anything again, perhaps for as long as he lived. And when the light came on and the turntable spun, Phil's head fell to one side, so as he rode the glass merry-go-round, his wide eyes looked out at Bobby as if asking if there was anything more to say.

Alabaster

Through the green and clear lake as you submerged, I could not tell the difference between your outline and an island. Your skin reminded me of alabaster. White, translucent. Your beauty spoke to me in the light passing through you and reflected by you.

There are only so many ways I can protect you.

There was such delight in your eyes when you found that carved, Mexican parrot at a barn sale up the Sixth Concession. The farmer must have been sitting there forever among the round bundles of greying hay, trying to sell it. I know how proud you were of it for the brief time it was yours, the same look you had in your eyes for the few hours we had our son. I failed to hold both tightly.

When I brought it out to show the neighbour you were talking to, and it slipped from my hands and shattered on the rock, I thought the world had broken.

Everything that should have wings is heavier than air. The instant the bird's short flight began, I knew it could not fly, and the hope went out of your eyes.

Now, as you swim, I know your eyes are open under water, looking for something that you once had and no longer see, and I cannot tell the difference between the lake and your tears.

The Tiptoe Effect

WE WELCOMED A bundle of joy into our lives and the thanks we got was that it grew teeth and bit us. It would bite us if we woke it up by not tiptoeing. We had to tiptoe around it at first, so it wouldn't wake. Waking it was bad. At first, it didn't have any teeth, but when we sat it in its vibrating chair, sometimes in the middle of the dining room table and sometimes in the corner of our bedroom, it would grunt and demand we pay attention to it. It made all sorts of demands, not by speaking or saying anything, but simply by being there and thinking its way into our brains until all we could think about was the bundle of joy.

The teeth it grew were sharp. If we thought it was asleep, we'd pry open its lips and see if it had grown more teeth, and it would snap its jaws shut on us. Shit, those were sharp teeth! They could chew clean through to the bone with one chomp. And it was getting more teeth. It would hold us hostage by crying and making impossible demands. Day and night, it kept up its insistence. We'd been warned, but we had no idea it would be like this. Then it began to grow.

It was still a bundle of joy, and it didn't stop being a bundle of joy, but as it became larger and larger, without any appreciable signs of changing into anything remotely human it started grabbing at things and breaking them. That's when we knew we had a problem on our hands.

By this time, the bundle of joy had grown so heavy we had trouble moving it from room to room, so we got a dolly, and pushed it with all our strength, and propped it in a corner of the living room. We didn't have many rooms, and the bundle of joy insisted on having its own space.

It made terrible smells, awful, noxious exhaustions that came from its mouth and other parts, and if we tried to help it out by cleaning it, it would bite us more, snapping its jaws shut on any part of us that came close enough to attack. And if we weren't careful, the bundle of joy would throw up on us or crap on us. Its crap could hurtle across a room if we weren't careful. We had to be very careful.

And it kept on reading our minds. If we even thought of something we wanted to do the bundle of joy would insist no and make us do something it wanted to do, most of which was stuff we had never imagined ourselves doing, stupid stuff, stuff that made us look like idiots if we did it in public. And we did.

It asked us to go out in the middle of the night if it had the craving for mushy food, especially mushy cod. All its food had to be mushy. And awful tasting. Once we tried tasting it. We tasted a spoonful of mushy cod. It was awful, and the bundle of joy caught sight of us making gagging faces at the taste of the mushy cod, and started screaming, telling us, telepathically and demonstratively that we had to lay off its mushy cod or else. It was frightening—not just the bundle of joy or its veiled threats but the mushy cod.

When we couldn't move it anymore, when it was way too

heavy to lift or shove or even reason with, it started wrecking the furniture. It would grab hold of a table and start chewing on the legs. It would roll over to a chair and gnaw on the rungs. It had to put every bloody thing we owned in its mouth. Everything the bundle of joy touched was gooey with slobber or mushy cod.

We thought we had it cornered in a part of the living room we rarely used, a part where our old stereo used to stand but that the bundle of joy had broken by pushing the buttons the wrong way, so all the old cassettes played at high speed and sounded like mice. The bundle of joy loved that. Good, we thought. We will play it the sound of singing mice to keep it happy so it won't bite us or spew on us and demand more mushy cod but that was short-lived.

One morning, when the house was quiet for the first time in ages, we fell asleep. We fell into a deep sleep, a sleep almost like death where we couldn't hear anything going on around us, and when we opened our eyes we were startled out of our wits. The bundle of joy was leaving.

It told us it wanted its own life, that it had learned to walk, and talk, and disagree not only with us but with the world, just like we used to disagree with the world when it got to us. It told us it loved us, sort of, and we had to admit that we had grown to love it too, not in the way someone loves an oppressive leader or a country with a restrictive regime but in an odd way we hadn't considered. We told it we loved it too, perhaps more than we cared to admit.

The door closed and our bundle of joy was gone. We weren't sure whether we had been saved or if a hole opened in our lives. We sat and drank our coffee on the living room couch and stared at the space where we had cornered the bundle of joy, and wondered how it all could have passed so quickly that we couldn't see what enormity the bundle of joy had been and how it had grown into something else when we thought we weren't watching and even when it was changing right before our eyes.

The Warm-Up

PEG TOLD HIM it was just the beginning.

There was enough snow outside to make a glacier think twice about sticking its nose beyond the doorstep. Peg knew her husband wasn't going anywhere. He'd have to walk three kilometers along the back trail to the flag stop. That kind of committed energy just wasn't in him.

She wanted to leave. She deserved to leave. Tom had been an ass all day, and she couldn't stand it anymore.

First, there had been the problem at breakfast. He'd complained about her eggs. He said there was cellophane around the edges. He hated cellophane. That should have been just cause to get up and walk out. It hadn't been snowing then, at least not as it was snowing now.

Then, around mid-morning, as she was working on her painting of the lake, a landscape with the heavy trees off in the distance and the outline of a moose on the far shore, he'd said the moose lacked empathy.

Empathy?

What in God's name was he talking about?

Who ever heard of an empathetic moose?

For crying out loud, they only see the world in black and white.

That's a fact, she'd shouted at him, but he didn't care. He, too, was seeing the world in only black and white. He was suffering from dispositional thinking.

But the worst came when she handed Tom a cup of tea just after noon.

He hadn't been hungry and said all he wanted was tea.

He asked her if she wanted her tea leaves read.

She didn't, but he read her future anyways.

He said she was going to leave him or him her. It didn't matter which. They were headed in opposite directions. That's when she snapped.

Now, he's outside in the snow. She turned his wounded head away from the window so she wouldn't be distracted when the moose came by and nudged him with its nose.

He just stares now.

How to Fold a Letter

THERE IS NO easy way to fold a letter. Granted, there is the old legal way his mother learned at secretarial school when she was young, unmarried, and working to save up for her dreams.

She did a great deal of dreaming in those days—thought about how she would meet the love of her life, imagined what sort of house they would eventually own, and entertained the idea of children, how many, what gender, and the sound of their voices. She knew that each time she folded a letter in the proper, legal way she was one message closer to making everything in her mind come true.

When her son was born, she wrote him a letter and folded it, not in the legal manner, but in a personal way, top to bottom, with the top tucked in as if she was settling him in his crib for an afternoon nap with a warm blanket drawn up around his chin. But she never sent that letter. It might embarrass him at the wrong time someday, she thought, if he opened it and didn't understand what she wanted to say to him.

She could not wait for the day when he would write his own letters, first to pen pals to collect stamps and learn of distant places, or later when he would put his thoughts to paper about the eyes of a girl who would become his first crush, and how they reminded him of stars captured in all their brightness in a photograph negative waiting to be printed.

After that, if he studied hard and put his mind to it, he would write to a college or university and request admission, then move away, perhaps calling her instead of taking the time to sit down and do a proper letter in his own hand; and she knew she could not keep a phone call in a box of memories the way she would a letter home. There would be nothing from him to read and reread in later years, but she would greet his calls and talk to him as if he was right there at the kitchen table or in the living room of their home with the television going in the background.

She would show her grown son, someday, the proper way to fold a letter if he came home for a visit between his work days and business trips, because merely opening a letter does not teach one how to fold it up again.

But he always called. And when he did come home, when he had found time in his schedule and noted it on his electronic calendar, she had forgotten the beauty she had always loved in a letter and simply sat with him in her living room, wondering what questions she should ask him as they listened to the sound of cars and buses in the street and knew they would not go too far away without someone knowing how they would return to the place from which they had been sent.

When We Are Not Here

IN A BLIZZARD, a person dies of invisibility. Other things—hitting a highway cut or a tree, skidding into a half-frozen swamp or colliding headlong with a transport truck—don't really enter the equation. They are all ways to die. But stalling out or pulling over during the worst of a storm, those minutes when only the hood of the car and the reflection of the headlights in the weft of flakes—that slow, patient, waiting as snow buries the car and the doors won't open and the exhaust gets covered over so that the car fills with the easy sleep from which there is no waking—that is what invisibility is all about. The fumes are invisible. The road ahead is invisible. There is nothing to see.

When we pulled over on our way north, Krissy told me not to get out of the car. We had to get to Sudbury. Her father was dying. I told her I thought we were in a hurry. She nodded. She knew she would not be there for the end, but under her breath she said something I could barely hear, something along the lines of one death that week would be enough. She was trying to be stoic. She was thinking clearly.

We should have pulled off at Parry Sound and tried to find a hotel for the night, phoned ahead and said we were caught in the storm that blew in off Georgian Bay, that the road was invisible and the snow was blowing sideways. Instead, we were sitting on the shoulder. The shoulder is not a good place to be. Someone can come along and hit you. Someone who hits you won't be able to see you. Being invisible is not a good thing.

By the time the battery died, we'd been on the shoulder for about four hours. I kept thinking there'd be a break in the storm. There wasn't. I'd forgotten all the dos and don'ts of winter travel. I'd left the car rug at home. I hadn't packed jerky sticks. Worst of all, the old boy scout trick of the candle in the tin can had slipped my mind. I'd left my cell phone to charge in the bathroom, and my link to the outside world gave our position as somewhere just south of French River. A smart winter traveller always carries road flares. I had held a box of them in my hand one September afternoon in Canadian Tire, but I thought they were too much of a hazard to drive around with. A boy in my grade four class had blown his right hand off with a fire cracker during a Centennial celebration. I was more frightened by fireworks and flares than of being invisible. I could imagine things that would do damage. I couldn't imagine invisibility.

Invisibility always goes hand-in-hand with stupidity. We live in the city and for some reason a tin can, a candle, and a lighter was an open invitation to vandals if we parked our car on the pad in the back lane. I had pictured our Ford Escort with flames leaping out the window and that had shut everything else I could have imagined out of my mind.

We'd had the radio on, tuned to a local station that kept issuing weather reports and travel advisories. Krissy was on her cell, but that died, and shortly after that the radio faded to silence. Then, the headlights went out along with the emergency flashers. Their red blinking through the snow would surely have signalled our presence. Now, that was gone, too. I kept wishing Krissy would get angry, would punch the dashboard, shout, swear, say something. But she was deep inside her own mind. She was preparing for the loss of her father. I don't know what she was seeing, but she was staring straight ahead at the snow-covered windshield. Her breath, as it curled from her mouth and nose, was beautiful. The windows were fogging over, and every small cloud of our presence froze on the glass until the inside surfaces were covered in a veil of ice. I put my thumb on my driver's side window, and the ice melted momentarily, leaving my thumbprint in the veil, before it refroze.

What goes through one's mind when one becomes invisible is a stream of pictures of a future that one may not be part of: the grey light of a morning, perhaps the next or the one after that, our bodies frozen, our eyes staring straight ahead, my hand almost in hers but hers pulled away in a gesture of refusal, the body language of a broken promise that says to those who find us that she is alone and doesn't care whether I am there or not.

Labour Day Monday

MAGIC MARK WAS standing in front of his car lot, white Stetson pulled low over his eyebrows to give him a tough hombre look as he recorded a new commercial. He was telling everyone that now that the kids were back to school he had a bevy—his word, bevy—of Buicks that needed to be schooled by great drivers, drivers who loved the smell of a new car and could teach it the ways of the road. He told everyone that he was open, and they ought to come on down for a hot dog. Mark's wife was sitting in a saran chair behind him and looked disinterested. There wasn't a line-up for the hot dogs. Hot air rising from the charcoal grill twisted like the mirage on a long road.

Everything was shut down as if it was Christmas. The banks, the liquor stores, the supermarkets—even the hospitals were on half-staff though the Emergency Wards would not turn anyone away. Labour Day was always the last gasp of summer before life roared back to life on Tuesday and reality returned from vacation. The day was meant to celebrate work, not encourage it. Families were supposed to attend picnics, some in parks thrown by unions, others simply backyard barbecues. The side streets filled with the smell of hamburgers cooking, but mostly an emptiness pervaded on the thoroughfares. It was as if a day set aside to celebrate work reminded everyone who ventured beyond their gatherings of what the world would be like if no one was there to keep it running.

Mark asked the cameraman if he could do the spot again, this time with his wife putting some condiments on a dog so he could make a joke about getting some mustard on a great deal, but the cameraman said he had to be somewhere and by the time he cut the piece to air on the eleven o'clock report, he'd be late. He had to be at a picnic somewhere before it started to get dark.

Inside the dealership showroom, Allan looked at his watch. Every Labour Day for the past five years, Mark had hired a new outsider—someone who wasn't a cousin or his wife's cousin, and every Labour Day for the past five years he had fired last year's outsider. Allan suspected that it was his time. He needed the work.

Mark approached the showroom like a baseball manager about to go to the mound. He had a walk that expressed whatever he was thinking. A saunter meant: "I'm going to make a deal but the sucker can wait." Or: "I'm going to fire a guy but he's got to watch me go through the motions." A hop meant: "No way, nothing doing, no deal." Allan knew that walk. Mark was about to tap his left arm the way a baseball manager signals for a change of pitcher. Mark's cousin, Ralphie, was sitting in one of the side offices with his feet up on the grey steel desk, his hands folded in his lap, and his eyes closed. Ralphie didn't hear Mark come in and wasn't aware that a customer had pulled into the lot.

Mark saw Ralphie and hollered at him, though Allan could not hear precisely what was being said as he slipped into the storeroom at the back of the dealership to check on the supply of floor mats. New floor mats were a bonus feature of every purchase. Allan emerged with a set of grey ones from the stock room and Mark asked him what he was doing.

"That guy there, the one who just pulled up. He's going to buy the grey sedan. See?" Allan laid the mats on Mark's desk and moved with his boss toward the window. "This one's mine," he said. "Watch this."

Allan went out to meet the customer. The customer was about thirty, wore a blue sport shirt, jeans, a broad belt, and had a good hair cut. Mark watched through the window with his arms folded as the customer started nodding and Allan nodded along with him to encourage him. It was a used Buick, about ten years old. Allan opened the hood. The customer leaned on the side as Allan pointed at the various parts of the engine, occasionally making a stirring motion or circling his palms in midair to indicate everything was working in unison as it should. This was the body language of salesmanship. All the while, they both kept nodding. Then they came inside. Allan showed the man to a chair in front of Mark's desk and took Mark by the arm to the storeroom.

"He's buying."

"Just like that?" Mark asked. "Whadya tell him?"

"He'd been watching the deal on Automart, and he's sold. He came in to inspect and buy. I'm closing, but not yet. He's asked for our special package—five hundred off the sticker and the floor mats."

"Oh, c'mon, really? He isn't dickering about needing two grand off the sticker and wanting undercoating and a bumped-up audio package?"

"Nope. He said his father had one just like it but the guy

died at the beginning of the summer and his mother misses having the car in the driveway."

"How did he die?" Mark asked.

"Wrecked his car."

"So, you're getting a deal from him on our deal and he's buying a goddamn ghost for his mother?"

"Sounds like it. I'm going to wait here for a few minutes, and then you're going to saunter out with me," Allan said as he sat down at the computer in his cubicle and Mark stood just inside the doorway. Allan typed away, hit the print button, and pulled the paperwork, signing his name, as the dealer of standing, at the bottom of several pages so his commission would be registered with the Automotive Dealers Association. Mark thought there was something about Allan that was off, something he hadn't noticed before in the months Allan had been on the lot, striking and closing deals. It was then Mark saw it. Allan was a southpaw.

"That's a quickie."

"He's got cash, too," Allan said, smiling. "Showed it to me while we were walking around the far side of the clunker. I'm not going to argue. Maybe he needs a getaway car or something, but cash is cash, right?"

"Yep," Mark said, pushing his cowboy hat back on his head.

The dealership owner and salesman emerged from the office. Allan sat down at Mark's desk and Mark stood leaning against it with his arms folded, as the young salesman went through the paper work with the buyer and Mark nodded to offer reassurance to both parties. It was that simple. Twenty minutes was all the deal took. Then the guy was off the lot. No wave goodbye. No farewell honk for good luck. No edge of the road rev of the engines. He just took off. The guy's wife had been parked in her car the whole time and drove away after her husband.

Mark sat staring at the stack of brownies—the total amount paid in hundred dollar bills, then held each one up to the light. "I'll be damned," he said, "they're all good."

"So," Allan said, "what now?"

Mark knew what Allan was anticipating. Mark got up from his swivel chair and paced back and forth. He took off his Stetson and ran his hand over the sweat of his bald head, then stopped and looked Allan in the eye. He hollered: "Ralphie? Get your fat ass out here."

Ralphie emerged from his cubicle, wiped the sleep out of his eyes and squinted at his boss.

"Hey Markie, I guess its Labour Day, eh?" Ralphie said, grinning and checking his pocket protector to straighten his pens with his right hand. "Dish it out, boss."

"Here," Magic Mark said, pointing to a spot directly in front of him so that Ralphie stood side by side with Allan. He looked at them both, sized them up, and as if he was signalling to his bullpen, tapped his left arm.

Hoodie

MY WIFE AND I enjoy danger, though maybe just a little bit. Sometimes we're too stupid to be afraid. Danger feels better when you aren't afraid and you don't read a moment as if it is dangerous. Like the morning two coyotes emerged from the ravine behind our house and ran through the neighbourhood in search of squirrels. The pair looked scrawny and hungry, circling trees, and checking under parked cars. I stood on our front porch with my wife trying to get a good picture of them.

Or the barn owl, a little grey, white, and brown fellow with big eclipse eyes who sat in our weeping cypress one autumn afternoon and stared at me until I got too close and it flexed its steel grey talons and raised one foot to show me the business end of his body. He just stared without blinking. Are owls psychotic? Maybe they are.

But those were good dangers. Natural perils. Pity the poor squirrels or someone who thinks the owl is cute and decides to feed it something stupid like a crust of bread or a dried dead mouse from the floor of the garage. Those are nature documentary kind of dangers. They don't seem real because they appear on regular television programs.

But the night we drove down our rear lane that ran between our backyard garage and the lip of the ravine, that was real danger. That's when we saw this black shadow. Too large for a cat, too undernourished to be a bear. I'd had a few drinks while we were out. My wife was doing the driving and she pulled to one side of the gravel track, and pointed saying: "Look, over there!"

I didn't see it at first. I was in a hurry to get in to catch the end of the game. I had ten bucks on my team. I didn't want to sit in the dark playing spot-the-weird-thing or whatever she wanted to do. I also had to use the can.

I was about to get out and open the garage door, but then it, the thing, the shadow, moved, crouching, and darted behind a truck belonging to the stonemason next door. We'd told him, every time we'd talk over the back fence, not to leave his truck in the laneway. He was a sitting duck. He'd lost a lot of tools, and the worst part was, he said, he'd show up on a job site expecting to start work and then have to drop everything and go to the big box hardware store and buy what he needed all over again. He was getting sick of it. And if he found the bugger who was taking his stuff, he'd clobber the guy with a piece of granite he drove around with all the time.

The shadow darted again, but this time toward the other side of our garage. It wanted to get away from our neighbour's truck. The cover was partly pried off the flat bed. A pick axe was lying on the ground. What would a shadow do with a pick axe? I wanted to jump out of our car, go over, pick up the axe and brandish it like a Viking and yell "Valhalla" in a deranged roar to let whoever was out there in the shadows understand, beyond a shadow of a doubt or a doubt in a shadow, that I wasn't to be messed with. And my neighbours weren't to be messed with. I wanted to defend something and do the defending violently, dangerously. Like an idiot. I wanted to be the defender of our laneway.

My wife reached an arm across to stop me from climbing out, saying: "Don't get out." But I saw the shadow, and I wasn't going to sit there watching our neighbour get ripped off. No way. I was up for the dangerous thing. Like photographing coyotes on a hunting mission or getting a close-up shot of a bird that could rip a vein from my neck. I got out of the car.

Then the shadow thing stood up. It was a teenager, maybe seventeen or eighteen—a boy, he could have been younger—it was hard to tell. He wasn't very strong looking. His hunch told me he was cold and hungry, but I was probably reading an element of helplessness into him. Helpless things are more dangerous. He had a jiggle bar in his left hand for opening car windows and in the other he held a knife. It wasn't a switch-blade. I would have understood a switch-blade. I would have thought: "Oh, he must be a tough from the local high school or part of a gang like Marlon Brando in *The Wild Bunch*." But no. The closest his knife came to being in a bunch of anything was likely a bunch of grapes or bananas. He disappointed me. It was a paring knife. The kind of knife I use on Sunday mornings for cutting my wife's grapefruit into slices. I should have been more frightened by it, but it wasn't frightening. It was for fruit.

He was wearing dark sneakers, black gym pants like the kind boxers train in to look tough. Rocky has on a pair when he runs up the steps of the art gallery in Philadelphia. And the shadow had on a black hoodie with the cowl up. Maybe he thought it was a kind of disguise, a half-hearted attempt to be a jiggle bar ninja in a laneway on the edge of a ravine, but the costume didn't work. He could have dressed as Batman and that might have been more dangerous. Superheroes are lunatics. But he had on white socks. Gym socks. The kind a person buys in a discount store, three pairs for a dollar. Guaranteed to last two squash games or maybe a week on a walking treadmill. Exercise socks. He tossed aside the jiggle bar and it jangled on the laneway's gravel.

He started walking toward me with the knife held out full length, like he had been told to be careful with it in case he fell on it. For a moment, I froze. I didn't know what to do. The kid had pimples. I thought: "I'm going to be killed by an acne case." Then I thought: "Yeah, guy, I can take you." I reached down and picked up a handful of gravel, grey stones about the size of robin's eggs, then stepped into the beams of our headlights.

He could have run. He should have run, but he didn't. No. The guy stepped into the lights, turned his face toward my wife in the glare so she got a good look at him, and he raised his hands over his brow and squinted at her.

That's when I thought about the coyotes. Hunting. Afraid. Struggling to survive. Maybe the kid was dying and he needed to rip off my neighbours. I thought: "Is there anything in my garage he would steal?" I pictured him slinking through the dark, pushing my lawnmower ahead of him, or maybe walking off with the spade over his shoulder, a shovel I had to use each spring for doing yard work. Or maybe my rake. I hate raking. I don't own any trees. The leaves belong to other people and I spend my time cleaning them up. My time.

Then my wife leaned on the horn. She blasted it hard. A long sound. A drone, baritone note like a train approaching a level crossing and seeing a van of nuns ahead, waving their arms in distress, pleading for the juggernaut to stop before it hits their charitable vehicle. Or at least it sounded like that in the darkness.

The kid dropped his knife, his bag, and ran into the ravine. I could hear him slipping and cursing as he hit things on the way down the embankment. I felt sorry for him. He was in a lot of danger. He could be breaking his leg. Then the crashing stopped.

As he disappeared, I heard a sound like two dogs howling at the moon, only much lonelier. And when my wife had shone the headlights in his eyes, they lit-up like two huge, lonely moons before the Earth moves its shadow between the lunar surface and the sun, glowing brightly, and then gradually going dark.

Snow Pudding

GEE WAS FROM up north and never understood directions in Toronto. Her extended family, most of whom had spent their entire lives in the city and would not leave it even in when their bodies had to be buried in the country plot they were entitled to, spoke the language of Toronto direction fluently.

They lived "*up* in the north end." The Viaduct was "*over* the Don," but the Danforth, not Danforth Road or Avenue, but just "*the* Danforth," was *out* east." So was Nova Scotia which was farther away than anyone could imagine from The Danforth, but if you went to Montreal on the train you were "*down* in Montreal." During the previous war, the boys had been "*over* in France," which in a manner-of-speaking was not far from the Beaches where one went "*down*" in order to have a picnic. But this war was different. The boys were "*off* in Hong Kong."

Gee said as she laid her knife and fork side by side on the empty plate of her Christmas dinner that "*off*" just wasn't right. "It is as if you are treating them like a lamp. On one minute, off the next. It doesn't bode well."

Martha, her sister-in-law, set aside the tomato jelly after helping herself and said: "It's a good thing they are '*off*' in

Hong Kong. The Japs aren't going near the place. They're too tied up in China, and now they've taken on everyone else in the Pacific. Hong Kong is a safe place for your Charlie."

Martha had decided to remember the boys, especially Charlie and his second cousin Don, by making their favourite desert. When the dishes were cleared away and the house was silent after the business of Christmas day, she would write and tell them both that they were in her thoughts and prayers, and spiritually evident in her snow pudding. She had saved her ration coupons and had been lucky enough to find five lemons. Mr. Taggert in the store said they were a head-scratcher when they arrived, by magic, from down in Florida. The Americans weren't sharing their fruit with anyone, except possibly Mr. Taggert.

The lights flickered as a sign that it was time to pull the blackout blinds. Annie, Martha's daughter, went around to each window and made sure that no cracks of light were seeping through or they'd get a fine.

"I've been doing civic defence at school," Annie said proudly.

Her father said: "You were on the roof of the bloody school doing plane spotting. I walked in and said to the principal: 'Look here, no daughter of mine is going to stand on your roof during an air raid. She's going to be safe at home in the coal cellar with me and her mother.'"

"He wants to go down to the coal cellar," Martha said to Gee. "We'd be black as night down there. We'd ruin our clothes, and washing supplies are getting so expensive these days. I think the army is rolling in too much mud, if you ask me."

Martha's husband stood up and went to the sideboard.

Just before he turned on the radio he asked if there was any more snow pudding.

"That last batch melted on my tongue. I don't know how you got the lemons, but it was perfect. I could just picture Lake Simcoe last summer, all of us eating out under the trees before we sent the boys off."

The radio, hushed at first, grew louder as it came to life. Martha's husband put his hand on the top to make sure it was warming up.

A voice emerged from the silence. "Here is the CBC News. Following a surprise attack on this holiday morning, the garrison at Hong Kong has fallen. Under a heavy Japanese invasion by land, sea, and air, the Empire forces defending the Chinese city, composed largely of Canadian troops, suffered heavy casualties before surrendering at 2 p.m. Ottawa time. In other news, Prime Minister King—"

Gee gasped. Martha raised her napkin to her eyes and began to weep into it.

"My poor boy," her husband said, "my poor, poor, boy."

"They might have gotten away. They might be safe," Gee said, though her voice was choked with tears.

But *off* was too far away to imagine. Annie, with tears in her eyes, tried to picture her brother. She stood at the drapes, her head bent and pressed against the window frame beneath them. She wanted to throw the curtains open, but instead peered into the backyard through a narrow slit. At first, she saw the reflection of her own eye, staring from the glass, trying to make out anything that might be alive and moving in the snow, but there was nothing there, and it would take a long time to melt.

Leash

SOME DOGS LOOK as if they don't know anything, but not a collie. Collies are always supposed to come to someone's rescue. A collie runs somewhere, and everyone knows that dog is on top of things, saving the life of someone who has fallen down a well. They are a credit to dogdom. Firemen in the city used to use collies to rescue people from burning buildings, but someone made them stop because collies are long-haired, catch fire more easily than short-haired dogs, and look terrible singed.

Allison didn't want to put out fires, but she wanted a collie. Her mother said their house was too small. It was. The house had two bedrooms, and because it had been built before the Second World War in what had been a working-class area of the city, the closets were shallow, just deep enough for three shirts—one to wear on Sundays or to be buried in, and the other two rotated in and out of service on work days until the cuffs and collars frayed. Her mother told Allison that the elderly couple who had owned the house before them had left a box of shirts in the basement, all with worn collars. Allison could have the pick of the litter for a painting smock or to play doctor in with the sleeves rolled up.

Collies and collars were the subjects Allison remembered

from her childhood. She imagined the perfect collie—long-haired, white, and black, and golden-brown—dressed up by her in a shirt with a frayed collar until the neighbour who owned Rexy told her to stop, saying dogs weren't meant to be dressed and it was insulting to them.

When Allison fell in love with Thomas, whose beard was long and golden brown, she would reach up and button the top of his shirt and he would ask her why. Allison didn't know. It was just something she loved to do.

Thomas was her pet.

Together they went for long walks along the river flats and back up River Street and through Little Chinatown if the weather was good. She would glance sideways at lamp posts and fire hydrants and hope they would have meaning for him, but they didn't. She told Thomas how much she had wanted a dog when she was a child, but her mother always pointed out their small house was no place for a dog because the closets were way too tiny.

On one of their walks, Thomas sat Allison down on a park bench in Withrow Park, and they watched the dogs running back and forth with their owners because the park was an off-leash area and the dogs had to learn to be friends. That's when he told her the truth about himself in his own way. He liked the dogs that lifted their legs on trees and fire-hydrants rather than the ones that had to squat.

"He probably just wanted his freedom," her mother said. "Men don't like to be on a leash, no matter how long you let it out."

Feeling as if no one would rescue her, Allison was inconsolable with her mother. The closets, she said, were not big enough for anyone to go into let alone come out of. She went to her room and wept as she held a dog collar. It was black, and silver and the name plate was inscribed "Thomas."

Top Six

Kaplasky used to stand in the dressing room before games and wave a jock strap and cup in the air and declare he was like Napoleon and was going to suit up like us. He said he'd know how we felt on the ice. One day, he didn't just hold up the cup: He dropped his pants and put it on, adjusting it and smiling. It was embarrassing seeing the coach's junk like that.

"Every game, men," he shouted at us as if he was a preacher full of the fury of the Almighty, "every game I will wear this, so I can get inside your heads and know how your brains work or not."

I wanted to tell him that I didn't let my little brain do my thinking for me on or off the ice, but he would have benched me. I was getting little ice time as it was, and I was the top scorer on the team.

We were the Roxboro Rovers. I don't know who the hell designed our logo. Some of the teams in our Junior B league had polar bears or vipers on their crests, and those were cool in a cartoon kind of way. Ours was a white rose. I mean, who the hell puts a rose on the front of a maroon jersey? On the white away jerseys you couldn't see the damned flower, and the other teams always told us we played like someone sprayed perfume on us.

We were never a good team.

We always sat at the bottom of the league, and I suspect that's why no one noticed Kaplasky for the seven years he ran our town's team. He'd pick his favourites. His favourites weren't the best players. At first, I didn't know why he chose the boys he did. Then I saw them either go into his office or come out. One day one of them was crying, a winger who should have been a fourth liner. The winger wouldn't say what had happened in the office and shoved me away.

We weren't a big town either. Roxboro was the kind of place you drive past because it's off the main highway six miles, and after the railway closed the line we weren't near anything except the town's rose garden where there used to be a bank.

It was my Mom who started the whole anti-Kaplasky thing.

I have a hockey mom. I love her dearly. She's the type of mom who drove me to practices at four a.m. through blizzards and sat in the stands with a stop watch. She calculated everyone's ice time. She showed us our Corsi ratings, time of possession, number of shots—the kind of stuff you'd expect from a major league statistics guru. No one asked her to do it. She just did it. She wanted me to get drafted, though she told me I'd be a late-rounder as long as Kaplasky was in charge.

Things fell apart for Kaplasky the day we lost thirteen to six. I had the six. Our goalies had the flu. Kap stood at the entrance to the shower room and kept grabbing his nuts, shaking them, and watching us. When you're showering with a bunch of guys, your teammates and your friends, guys you go to high school with, the kind of mates you stick up for in school, you don't stare at their junk. Really, there's no place one ought to look. So, I looked at Kaplasky.

He was holding a long-stem white rose, sniffing it, shaking his cup—at the time I thought he had a cup on—and yelling at us, telling us we were thorns. Then he threw the rose down on the tile floor of the shower and told us none of us were men enough to pick it up from the suds. So, Gary, the winger who'd come crying out of Kap's office, bent down and got it, his ass facing Kaplasky, when the oddest look came over the coach's face and he turned and disappeared into his office. Gary wrapped the towel around his waist and followed Kap behind the closed door.

I wrapped a towel around my own waist, my hair dripping on my shoulders, and followed him in my thongs. I wanted to see what was happening in there. Usually, if a coach is going to yell at you, you're allowed to get dried and dressed first. When I opened the door to his office, Kap had his trousers down and he was cleaning himself up.

I said: "Hey, how come I score six goals and I don't get more than ten minutes in a game? Do you even know what kind of Corsi that says about me?"

"Close the door," he said. "You can be top six if you want." And just as he was about to zip up his pants, he stopped, dropping them. I turned and left, but as I stepped out of his office, I pushed a chair against his door. My Dad was standing outside the entrance to the change room as one of our goalies slammed the locker room door open, and everyone in the hallway outside could see Kaplasky with his junk hanging out, Gary crying in a heap on the floor, his towel to one side, and that's when the investigation started.

So, by the next weekend, there was a guy from the league

standing in our dressing room, a bunch of lawyers, the top six guys having been questioned, and the rest of us sitting in the dressing room wondering whether we should suit up or not. The Vipers were already skating their warm-up.

The guy from the league shouted: "Listen up! Guys, you're forfeiting today's game."

Someone yelled "Shit!" because we still had a chance, remote as it was, to make the playoffs if we didn't lose any more games.

"The team is being disbanded. It's in debt and you no longer have a coach."

"What's going to happen to us?" I asked.

"We'll have a dispersement draft and you'll have to go where we send you." That meant that if we wanted to continue playing hockey we'd have to move away from home. I was prepared to do that. I got picked by the Vipers. I was their top scorer in the playoffs and got noticed enough to get chosen by a Junior A team, and eventually I went in the third round of the big draft. I did a couple of years in the ECHL, then I thought, what's the point? The guys there, at that level, staring up at the big leagues like fish with lights on their heads at the bottom of a sea trench—I'd have to get past them if I ever wanted to be a success.

Our top six didn't get chosen in the dispersal draft. Those six, all of them ... I'd like to say I knew what became of them, but hell, who knows. No one in Roxboro ever mentions the team. They tore down the arena to put it all behind them. The rose garden was dug up for a parking lot.

When I was skating for one of those southern ECHL teams, a franchise in the middle of Alabama with a mildly inappropriate logo that recalled the days of the Confederacy

—the Rebels—I was certain I saw Gary. I was boarding the Stars and Bars bus for a long ride to Florida. Gary was sitting slumped on the sidewalk outside a greasy spoon that had closed for the night. His left sleeve was rolled up past his elbow and his right hand was open with a syringe in the palm. And in his other hand, he held a limp white rose.

What Kasha Said

I LIKED KASHA. She had brown eyes that said much more than any words she ever used. Her eyes could comment on things that could not be said in awkward circumstances. I became intrigued by her eyes during a Medieval History tutorial, and she saw me looking at her. That's how we met. I had assumed she was English, possibly Welsh because of her dark hair. Her accent was British but that was only because she had spent the early part of her teens in Guildford before her family moved on, but though it was brief it was enough to make her sound British to those she knew.

Her first language was Albanian. Her father had been a junior minister in the Nazi-puppet government during the Second World War, and when the Hoxha Communists took over, Kasha's mother, father, and eldest sister were given refuge in Franco's Spain. That's how the family came by Spanish, but during the war, to appear chic among the powerful members of the political elite, they had spoken Italian at home whenever possible. When they moved from Madrid to Brazil, where Kasha was born, her first language was neither Spanish, nor Italian, nor even Albanian as one might assume, but Portuguese, which she said she spoke terribly, though she often broke into a mixture of Italian and Albanian at home to make herself understood to her parents who had become lost in the household Babel. Her older sisters scolded her in Spanish and she said she had to stick up for herself in Franco's lingua franca because she was fluent in the two languages the others struggled to speak, Portuguese and English.

I brought her to a family gathering when we had only been dating for two weeks. That was a bad move. My uncle, a very bigoted former air force officer from the war, leaned over to my mother and asked: "She isn't Catholic, is she?" My mother turned and looked floored at him.

"No," she said. "She isn't. I think she's possibly Australian." My uncle nodded in relief. My mother hadn't lied. Kasha was Muslim but knew enough of the Book of Common Prayer from her Guildford days to pass muster with my uncle when he quizzed her on Church of England rites. I intervened. The nerve of him. Interrogating her like that. Later, when I was taking her home, I apologized.

"It's nothing," she said. "It's a big world we all rattle around in. I'm the product of a family that has been shaken but not stirred, as James Bond would say." I smiled and nodded, and I could see she was happy with my attempt at contrition when I looked in her eyes.

We had begun meeting up. I wouldn't call it dating. She would call me from her home with strict instructions that I wasn't to call her at her number. If I wanted to contact her, I had to leave notes at the library sorting desk where she worked part-time to pay her tuition. Her home life, she said, was something she never discussed with people. When I asked why, she said it was because her family had moved around. Changing addresses was how they stayed safe. Her father had died in Brazil. Her mother blamed the Communists, and said the family would never know peace because of the red terror. But the death of Kasha's father had made her mother even more of a Fascist than when she had stood at her husband's side during the war and watched the Axis armies crumble before the partisans.

"And why did your mother want to come to Canada?"

"You'd expect me to say for her children's education," (Kasha had three sisters and two brothers, and I wondered what they lived on, let alone how all of them had put themselves through university), "but the truth is she thinks she's being hunted by Albanian agents." She must have seen me look askance at her because she added: "Really. She thinks they're standing across the street. She thinks they're everywhere. She might even think you're one if I didn't introduce you properly."

And when I finally met her mother, we were not properly introduced according to the multilingual customs of her home. I had pulled a two-and-half-day essay writing session. It was the end of the term and when I arrived at Kasha's house—we had planned to go out for ice cream and walk along the Kew Beach Boardwalk which I had never seen—she showed me in to her living room, said her mother was out and that I should wait on the chesterfield while she put on a fresh black sweater. I think I fell asleep.

I woke. Kasha had slipped beside me, draping my arm over her shoulder, and falling asleep against my chest with my denim shirt bunched in her left hand. It was the image of perfect innocence until her mother stepped into the room and screamed. There was shouting. I heard some words I understood and others that were completely foreign to me. Kasha's eyes were tearing and red as she pointed to me, then her mother, and threw out the palms of her hands in desperation. The mother had intense brown eyes, even more intense than Kasha's and anger turned them into the dark centres of storms. They wanted to burn a hole through me. I could feel it.

Kasha and I sat on a bench on the boardwalk and stared at the lake. Some gulls were hovering over bread crusts left on the sand at the water's edge.

"You know, there isn't really a tide here, at least not much, so I've been told."

"You don't need to make filler talk," she said. "I know this can't go any further. I really like you, but my mother told me that if I didn't come back in an hour I would not be able to come back at all. My older sister, the one you've never met—she never came back. I can't do that."

"I'm sorry. I understand, I think."

"It is more complex than you know," she said as she stood and was about to bid me farewell.

"Before you go," I said, "there's something I need to know."

"Please don't."

"No, it isn't about us breaking up. It is about while we were on the sofa. I woke up before your mother came in. I was listening to the noise of the street. Some kids were playing down the block. And then you said something. You were dreaming, but you talked in your sleep. A psychology prof I had in first year said that our real language, the one that is our true mother tongue, is the one we dream in. Although there were one or two words you were saying that I thought I could understand—bicycle was one of them—I couldn't figure out what you were saying, what your heart's language is.

What language do you dream in? It's an odd question, but I need to know."

Kasha smiled, though her eyes told me she was brokenhearted. "Me? Inside me? I have made up my own language. I am the only one who speaks it. It is not made of any of the tongues that have shaped my life. It is my own way of telling myself what I feel because I can't say it, no matter where I am or who I am speaking to. And you, well, you're the only one, other than me, who has heard and tried to understand."

The Sophomore Philosophy Club

IT WAS SUPPOSED to be role-play night for the Sophomore Philosophy Club, but it went south very quickly. Schopenhauer had gotten the whole thing off to a bad start by asking Heidegger for twenty dollars, which Heidegger obliged because it suited his theory of linguistic interrogation, thinking that, at last, the old question of Schopenhauer's coin on the tavern table would be put to rest because he'd have to pay up. But Schopenhauer shoved the bill in his mouth, and Hume argued that Schopenhauer didn't know where the bill had been, or who had handled it, and the whole business was uncertain, if not questionable *ad extremis*. Besides, shoving money in one's mouth was disgusting.

Spinoza who had been watching everything through a large magnifying glass he'd brought with him as a useless prop for the evening said: "Well, that's the last you're going to see of that twenty." And then turned to Schopenhauer and said: "You're an idiot, you should have asked for a brownie or a sunburn," meaning, according to Berkeley who hastened to explain that a sunburn was a fifty and a brownie was a hundred, that all the money in the world was actually inside him and he just had to find it for himself. But Heidegger didn't get the connection between the slang term for large denomination Canadian bills and thought that Spinoza was telling him to eat shit, and that's when the fight began.

Heidegger lunged at Hume, but Hume stepped out of the way because he understood the fundamentals of human nature and saw the anger coming, but in doing so tripped over Plato and spilled Nietzsche's beer. Nietzsche, Hume was certain, threw the first punch, but it was Russell who took it on the chin as Plato tried to dodge the fray and fell backwards into Anselm. Anselm knew there might be trouble as he'd had an *a priori* premonition that philosophy could get out of hand, even at the undergraduate level, and pulled a hammer out of his backpack, screamed "God!" at the top of his lungs, whirled around, and caught Nietzsche in the side of the head which made him cross-eyed for a second, just like the real Nietzsche who appears on page 365 in *Understanding Philosophy* by Hunter and Hoote. At this point, Nietzsche, covered in blood and beer, staggered forward with his fists flailing and took out Plato who fell squarely into Socrates who was sitting there asking: "What the fuck's going on?"

The two Greeks fell to the floor—Aristotle had known enough to retreat to a safe corner in the room where he could get a better definition of what was happening. Socrates fell on Nietzsche's glass and opened up a huge wound in his hand. He stood up, looking at the blood, and said: "Why am I bleeding?" Hume and I (I'm Leibniz) looked at him and said: "Know thyself." To which Hume added: "The unexamined hand is not worth shaking." And we decided to get the hell out of there. Nietzsche was heard hollering at Aristotle: "I'm going to make a tragedy out of you," as we headed down the hall on our get-away.

A little guy, who was supposed to be Machiavelli but who was late for the real-politick of the evening, met us on the stairs. He was lugging a two-four, and I said: "This is the best of all possible worlds." And Hume said: "That's cheating, you're parodying yourself." And I said: "Well, hell, why not? There's more beer there than we can put back in an hour." So the three of us headed off to the park down the street from the dorm.

Machiavelli, Hume and I were joined under a large maple tree by Aquinas who had gotten out via the fire escape. "You know," Thom said philosophically, "I can't make any order out of what's going on in there."

Hume took a long chug of beer. "It is human nature," he said. "Just human nature."

"No, I beg to differ. I think it is perfect. It is the expression of the monads that govern the universe, the beauty that makes each leaf on every tree a work of mathematical perfection. Beer is also mathematical perfection." We clinked our bottles.

We sat for the next several hours beneath that maple tree. A soft breeze was blowing under the leaves and rustling them in the night. The campus police were busy breaking up the Sophomore Philosophy Club in the dorm ... the entire fourth floor had become engaged, engineers battling with psychologists, battling with historians, and so on.

After a long silence, Thom said with a sigh: "You know, that's what's fucked up the Western mind. There's no fucking arguing with the world but that's what all this philosophy bullshit is about. I'm switching my major next term to literature. At least by the time I get to the last page of a novel I'll know how it ends, and there's always that blank page after the final one. That scares the shit out of me, but it makes a pretty profound statement. I always draw a sunset on it, and a cowboy with his back to me, just to ease my anxieties."

And as he said that, I pictured cowboys riding off into the postcard perfect sunset with silhouettes of mesas rising around them in the afterglow like the last scene in the *Magnificent Seven,* and considered how we might have saved the village if we'd given it some thought.

The Run

IN A GOOD week of summer weather, my team could lay a run of five blocks or more. First, we'd start by tearing up the old sidewalk, usually early in the morning when people would holler out their windows at us, tell us what sons of bitches we were for starting at that ungodly hour. I wanted to remind them that progress doesn't take prisoners and they should be up and at it if they wanted to seize the day. Our foreman Frank was usually the guy to tell them that. We weren't permitted to exchange words or blows with the people on the street. It was against company policy.

Rain was always a problem. If you're going to lay a run of sidewalk, you can't have rain. The bed beneath the new cement has to be level and dry or else the run will heave once the frost comes. When a run heaves, it cracks, and then we're back again in the spring to fill in the cracks in the slabs or just tear them up and start all over. Sidewalks are like the funeral business, in that respect. You never run out of work. There's always something ahead of you to get to.

If you walk along a street in the north end of the city, especially, you can almost figure out how many times it rained the year the sidewalk was laid. The slabs, as required by civic bylaws, must have date stamps, and you can tell by how often the date stamp changes whether it was set in a wet year or a dry year. You can also tell the good years from the bad by how often the dates change. A good year should last forever, with its date intact, like a tombstone.

We got to this one street where the sidewalks looked like a damaged cemetery. The surfaces were worn and cracked. You could see the slurry of small pebbles that pocked the surface as the smooth covering disappeared. But there was this one stretch, a run set in 1923 that hadn't seemed to age. The slabs were almost good as new. We knelt down and ran our hands over the surface because we'd never seen such immaculate sidewalks. 1923 must have been a good year. But we had to start the demolition anyways. Company rules. Take up the old, lay down the new.

I started with a jack hammer at the eastern corner. I chipped away all morning and nothing changed. The slab was there. We stood around during our break and discussed what we ought to do with 1923. We concluded that we should pry it up with crow bars. Someone asked about the rest of the run. Those pieces were going to be just as difficult. The framer came up with the idea that a fork-lift with long prongs—his brother just happened to have one and could come in an hour—could get underneath the run and simply flip it over. So, that's what we did. His brother came around with a truck and the forklift worked just like a bobcat. Our bobcat was somewhere else when we needed it.

We'd just finished lunch. The foreman came around and asked why we were buggering off. We told him about 1923. "That's the damnedest thing," he said, removing his construction hat and wiping his bald head with a red handkerchief. "Damnedest thing."

But the real damnedest thing happened when we flipped the slabs. Nothing had even shifted them for almost a century, and when they flipped, we found coins people had tossed into the cement mix. Coins in a mix are supposed to be lucky. The pennies were shining. We found a newspaper rolled up. It was from July of the year and it was in good shape—good enough to read. But the part that really freaked us was when we were sitting on a lawn and people, real people, not ghosts, not spirits, not phantoms from the overheated brains of men who'd been out in the sun all day, but real people, started emerging from the run. One man, a guy in a three-piece suit and bowler hat, came up to me and asked how far it was to number 231. I pointed down the block and he thanked me and went on his way. A girl in a white dress with puffed sleeves, the kind of kid you see in old movies, especially silent films, came skipping out of the earth. I know we weren't supposed to speak to the people on the street.

"Hey kid," I hollered, "how long have you been under there and watcha doing down in the ground?"

"What do you mean?" she asked, and I pointed to the run we'd just torn up. She began to cry, sobbing softly at first, and then breaking into a full wail.

"Why are you crying, kid, don't cry." One of the guys reached into his lunch pail to see if he could find the bear claw his wife packed for him every day to give him an extra boost in the afternoon.

"It was my mark," the kid said. "It was all that was left of me in the world. And you've broken it. You've torn it up." She was holding a doll. The doll's right hand, just like her right hand, was grey with dried cement. "We left our mark on the world. It was the only thing anybody remembered about me, and now it's gone."

I turned to the guys. We had to do something. The kid was freaking us all. So, we went to the first slab of 1923, the one that seemed so important to her, and flipped it over. There was the hand print we hadn't noticed, and the miniscule handprint of her doll.

"Okay, kid," I said, "we have two options. We can have you set your handprint in the new slab or we can re-lay the old one with your mark on it."

"Both," she said through her sobs. "I want both."

The entire team struggled to set the old slab in place. We figured if we laid it so it lined up with the new work, it would fit right in and the inspector wouldn't notice. Kids aren't supposed to write their names in fresh concrete, especially not the city's concrete, but that's never stopped them, or their dolls. We'd see it on just about every job. We hated it when someone wrote fuck or shit in our work because that was defacement, that was a sign they denigrated our work. In the autumn, a leaf would settle on the soft batter and its imprint would remain like a small miracle. I always thought leaf prints were kinda nice. But a kid's hands? That's innocence. That's gotta be preserved for posterity or something. I mean, look at the world. We need to be reminded that there's innocence and it's important.

As we smoothed over the freshly laid batter, raking in the grooves to keep people from slipping if it got icy, tamping in the edges so the new slab had a nice frame, and finally setting the city's official date stamp in the mix, the kid bent down with her doll and they made their prints. I should have asked her name. I didn't. And I'll never know.

What I did know was that people become the paths they walk every day. They are swallowed, without knowing it, in their familiar ways, in the routes they trace without giving a second thought to whether they are going home or going to work, or just walking around the block to clear their minds, or whether they'll ever come back to that place. They are prisoners of familiarity, just as I have become a prisoner of familiarity to the point where I can tear up and lay down a sidewalk in my sleep; and when I close my eyes, I see the mix being poured into the pegged frame. I see my paddle stirring it, smoothing the surface with what we call a float, and then walking away. I imagine my life as sidewalks I tear up and lay and never have a chance to walk because they have not set by the time I board the company truck and leave. When I die, I don't want to be trapped somewhere. I want to say I've had a good run and leave it at that. Maybe many good runs, but that's a cement man's joke.

Just as the man in the three-piece and bowler hat had asked for 231 and then disappeared, the kid was only present for a short while. We didn't see where the man had gone, but the kid—maybe it was magic or maybe it was just the way the place had become all she was and all she would ever be—the slab, the old one we'd reset reached out and drew her back into its mystery, down in the ground where the past goes because it has nowhere else to live.

Warts

I HAD MY first boyfriend and I knew my father didn't like him. My father would stand at our front window, sometimes with binoculars, and watch us walking through the park across the street. My boyfriend earned my father's dislike on their first meeting. He told my father that poetry was a useless. My father is a poet. Not just the modern kind with the beard, but the ancient kind, the spooky kind.

I've been to my father's readings. He goes from English into Gaelic as if someone inside merely flipped a switch. He's a poet who can make flowers appear out of thin air or pull coins from people's ears. He haunts them. My boyfriend humoured me by coming to a reading. I got to hate poetry too.

Things came to a head when my boyfriend started writing bad limericks on the tile in our washroom. He used erasable ink, but that didn't matter. My father saw it as mockery, especially when Nantucket became involved. That's when things began to change between my boyfriend and me.

One day he showed me his palms. They'd grown hairy. My father met him at the door, looked at the hands and said: "I know what you've been doing, ha, ha."

Then the warts appeared. They grew on my boyfriend's

lips, then his eyes. He stopped seeing me, but I stood outside his house and sang to him of love and beauty. I blessed him with the sun and moon. He wrote me a letter. *You are my poetry*, was all it said.

Edible Flowers

As I BOWED my head and closed my eyes during the final prayers for the old woman, all I could see were pansies. My grandmother adored them—she grew them from seeds in window boxes in her kitchen, from tiny pots in her bathroom, and in old Oil of Olay jars in her bedroom, starting them in the thin rays of February light and coaxing them into being when they were ready to be planted in early May when the snows cleared. Her yard was a riot of Johnny Jump-Ups that spread from the flowerbeds and wove themselves into the fabric of the lawn and the cinder path from her back porch to cobwebbed garage. I saw them—the pansies, yellow, blue, red, orange, and all the purple, white, and yellow Johnnies—when I closed my eyes after hours of tending her garden as she watched out her bedroom window. She had grown too frail to work the flower beds and had asked me to come and sort the first flowers of spring from a wild mess into a ribbon of blossoms astride the path.

When I was a child, I would go to stay with her. She would prepare lunches of egg salad sandwiches and tomato jelly served on a bed of lettuce. Scattered in the sandwiches, windfallen over the lettuce, and set in the jelly, were pansies and Johnny Jump-Ups. Each plate she served me was a garden. The first time my lunch blossomed, I was not sure what to do.

My mother had warned me not to eat anything I found outside. My mother grew petunias, and I was told they would make me sick. But after some coaxing, my grandmother persuaded me to taste the blooms. Johnny Jump-Ups are mildly peppery. There is an after taste of something I have never been able to describe properly—not spice or pepper, but something far gentler that speaks to the mouth with a touch of colour, if that's the way to explain it. Pansies are far more emphatic in their taste. They declare themselves with a brisk, slightly bitter presence like endive. I once tasted tiger lily shoots. They taste like pansies.

Taste is the most difficult of all the senses to put to words. Every experience in the mouth has to become a simile, because nothing is like itself; everything is like something else. Language has its limits. There aren't enough words to put in one's mouth, and that has always bothered me as the great deficiency of vocabulary: What lives in the mouth and comes from the mouth is its own silence, its own reticence to know itself. If the hardest thing to imagine is the self, then taste is the hardest thing to describe because it sits on the tongue, masking the words I want to find to explain what I know is there.

But then, there are violets. They, too, appear during the first days of spring. They, too, refuse to be held behind border rows of bricks or petite flower bed fencing. They rise out of the lawn. A violet, unlike the other first flowers of spring, loses its shape, its unique crispness and individuality the moment it is picked. The brevity of a violet is its beauty. In

Charlie Chaplin's *Modern Times*, a blind girl sits on the street corner and sells the Little Tramp her violets. Perhaps her tiny hand is frozen, like Mimi in *La Bohème*. The problem with her violets is that their perfume is almost lost the moment they are picked. A bouquet of violets is a small handful of echoes of a time and a place where death rules everything in the world except the life that resists in violets.

On my summer vacation when I was three, I stood in the waves with my grandmother. We sang "Ring Around the Rosy," and I had no idea that "pocket full of poesy" consisted of violets to ward off the smell of death from the plague. It would have seemed wrong to explain that to a child, as we laughed and bobbed in the shallows and the waves rolled in and splashed our shoulders. To taste a violet, however, is a very different experience from tasting pansies. Violets do not taste as much as they leave an aroma in the mouth, a lingering sensation that a perfume has entered past the lips and nose and created a beauty that is an expression of taste and scent.

In London, Fortnum and Masons produce chocolates that are flavoured with violets. The cream candies are sweet, aromatic, but the taste is ethereal. On top of each sweet sits a candied violet petal glistening in small crystals of sugar. The taste is sweet, but there is something else, something beneath the sugar that wants to be remembered. I brought my grandmother a box of the violet creams when I visited London on a high school tour. I remember her biting into one, closing her eyes, and saying: "Ah, the taste of springtime."

I had just finished sorting my grandmother's garden when I was called inside the house by my mother. My grandmother had been ill during the final months of the winter. I had thought that the coming of the warm days would give my grandmother her strength again. She had, just days before, sat in the sunlit window of her bedroom, her eyes closed to the warm light on her cheeks. When I looked up from the yard work and saw her outlined by the drapes, I imagined she was dreaming of pansies. They were almost ready to plant. The flat broad leaves of the violets had already emerged from the thatch of brown grass, and the Johnny Jump-Ups had sent up small, green shoots as the first sign that they were willing to continue with their brief lives. I imagined May giving way to June, thought about what I would plant among her perennials of Sweet William, Delphinium, and Cosmos. I had examined the rose bushes I had cut back in the autumn, and saw delicate green nubs fighting their way through the tops of the stems. And I tried to remember how rose petals taste when they are candied and flavour the cream chocolates she loved. This year, I thought, I will plant a bush for her. It will be a long-stemmed red rose and its perfume, the delicate scent that hovers over saints whose flesh will not go back to the earth, will help her hold on to life, even as the petals open wider and wider and fall to the ground.

Popcorn

"THEY TEACH US how to dream," Aunt Elizabeth would say as we walked along the west-end street near her apartment and joined the ticket line at the Seaforth. "Life can have a different ending, the Hollywood happily ever-after, not just the one that circumstances dish out."

When she told me that, I was too young to understand, but each time she would take me home after our outings and say goodbye, she would turn on the front walk, wave to me as I stood in the open door, and say: "See you in the movies."

At the Seaforth, as she leaned into the round, silver speaker of the ticket booth, she would clutch the heads of her fox stole and slip the dollar bills through the portal of the ticket shelf. "One adult, one fine, young man," she would enunciate so the ticket lady could hear her through the slatted chrome speaker.

The marquee was lit with bulbs that illumined the cinema name and the title of the feature, as if a chain of angels danced around a beloved saint. After we'd paid the woman in the glass booth, a man in a round pill-box hat and a short, red, military jacket piped in fraying gold gimp tore our tickets in half and then saluted us with two fingers raised to his forehead. Beyond the plush, brocade carpet, gold art deco columns rose to hold brass bowls that resembled torches either side of the main door. Flights of sweeping stairs guarded the wings of the foyer, and everything smelled of popcorn.

She had seen the features when they came out, but by the time Aunt Elizabeth began taking me to the pictures, the Seaforth was a rep cinema and played the old reels until they jammed in the sprockets of the projector and burned to a blinding white light. In the pauses when the projectionist spliced the pieces together and the house lights came up, she would turn to me and quiz me about the film until the lights dimmed again and the movie resumed. Her final words in the darkness were always: "They don't make them like that anymore."

My Aunt Elizabeth was a war-bride and a war-widow all within a matter of weeks. She never remarried. She was passionate about movies. They filled her life with a romance and glamour that was but a shadow on the screen but real in her mind. If she loved a film, she would sit through it a dozen times, and I would glance at her in the darkness as she mouthed the words with the script.

She adored movie heroes. They may have been the image of the beloved she lost and never mentioned. I wanted to be her new hero. I admired movie heroes, too. On the way out through the lobby, we would pause in front of the cardboard posters mounted on brass easels at the theatre doors and she would tell me how I resembled Van Johnson or Richard Todd.

The first movie I saw was Walt Disney's *The Sword in the Stone*. It tells the story of a young boy named Arthur who no one believes when he pulls a magical sword from a stone. "Only a king could perform such a feat of strength," the cartoon knights tell him. But he knows what he could do, and when he produces the sword for the peers in the tavern, they tell him he is a liar. Arthur takes the knights to the stone, reinserts the blade, and draws it out again. He was meant to be a hero.

After the house lights dimmed to a frail glow, I could still see shadows cast on the brocade-covered walls. The ushers, also in pillbox hats and waist-length red jackets, had flashlights. The rear doors were padded burgundy leather which was held in place with polished bronze nail heads. Rows of plush velvet seats, the quiet hush of movie-goers waiting for the show to begin, reminded me of sitting in church on Good Friday evening where the faithful waited, as if in the belly of a whale, for an act of faith—the return of light and life.

With the first ray from the projection room high behind us, I felt more awe and reverence in a movie theatre than I did at the moment of holy awakening. When I told Aunt Elizabeth what I thought of movie theatres, she scolded me and told me she would not take me to any more shows if I spoke blasphemy. I didn't know what blasphemy was, but I understood that holiness took many forms. Church was church, she said, and movies were movies and the two should never be confused for each other. They are separate realities, both wonderful and mysterious in their own ways, and both worth the price of admission. To me, though, a full-length feature contained as much ritual as a mass.

When Aunt Elizabeth was dying, I would check to see what was playing so we'd have something to talk about while she waited for the inevitable darkness. Sometimes, if the movie was one of our favourites, I would buy a ticket for the almost-empty house. The silence reminded me of the silence in her respite-care unit late at night. The only difference was that, after the momentary darkness, the screen would light up with a preview of coming attractions and the feature would begin.

Our lives are bound to the dreams we make, I told myself the last night I went to the Seaforth. Like an old faded print that had been run through a projector too often, the soundtrack from the movie sounded muffled as if the actors were speaking under water or from a far away place in another time. Our Seaforth had been splendid once, but as it fell into decrepitude, the sloping floor of the orchestra became covered in chewing gum so every step was laboured, and springs poked through some of the striped plush cushions. I thought I understood what made the movies, our movies, great, but when I sat in the darkness waiting for the final show to run, I realized the greatness was not the stars or the soundtrack, the costumes or the dances. What made the movies great were perfect stories about lives that sought happiness in a world determined to stifle joy. And every time, without fail, a movie offered a moment of hope, a great closing monologue, a vision of a brighter tomorrow that reached through the fifth wall to draw us in and from reality something in us was redeemed. They fed our imaginations so we could go on living. What made movies great was the strength of our own dreams.

On that final night, the air from the Seaforth's loges that once smelled of teenagers' perfume and cigarette smoke now seemed stale as if no one breathed it anymore, not even between kisses. But the lobby still smelled of popcorn, and the gold curls and leaves woven into the lobby carpet still wanted to speak of grandeur. The glass booth out front had been boarded up, and the terrazzo entrance that bore an elegant brass SC set in a mosaic was cemented over. The kings and queens of the silver screen no longer dwelt in their palace.

On my last night at the Seaforth, the house was empty except for me and an old man who had fallen asleep in the back row. The ushers, the ticket takers, the woman in the glass booth, were long gone. The rainy night had likely kept most people away. No one wanted to be bothered with the old films or thought them important enough to spend a few hours in the dark. Most people had probably seen *Sunset Boulevard* sometime in their past and didn't bother to make the time to see it again. It was available on Netflix.

"I'm still big," Gloria Swanson says as she looks directly into the camera. "It's the movies that have gotten small." And when William Holden falls into the swimming pool near the end, and floats, face-down like Jay Gatsby, I felt as if part of me no longer believed in the power of illusions, though I longed to pull the proverbial sword from the stone, and prove, if only for a moment, I could be a hero to someone.

As I passed through the lobby, the door to the payphone box was open for someone to pull the mahogany louvre closed and drop in a dime—now two quarters—and hear the phone chime before turning the rotary dial. It was late, but I wanted to tell Aunt Elizabeth that the Seaforth was still alive, as alive as the illusions it once held, and that a beam of light still flooded the darkness with the sound of a clacking projector behind me and the voices of adventurers ahead of me.

When they put me through to the nursing station and I asked how Elizabeth Starling was doing, there was a pause, a mumble of voices in the background, and they told me she had slipped away that evening. I sank low in the narrow booth, until I came to rest on the wooden misericord that every phone booth once had, and wept. I held the receiver in my hand at the end of its long, black cord. A voice from the earpiece kept asking if I was there. I couldn't say anything. I kept imagining that it was all a twist of plot, and that I would see her in the movies, in a scene where a boy and an old woman rush through a rainstorm to buy their tickets for a journey to another world.

Rec Room

WE LOVED THE name of it. Rec short for recreation, of course, but it could also have been wreck if we wanted to spell it badly. The rec was our place. We lived by our own rules there or thought we did. A re-creation room. A place to recreate ourselves. It was big in the Fifties and Sixties. A hang-out. It was a place to put up our Christmas tree at the one time of year our parents ventured into that part of the basement. At Christmas we had to celebrate the coming of the baby Jesus but other times of the year we could say *Jesus* if something was stupid.

One day, my sister who is very astute, turned to me and said: "Jesus. Isn't it blasphemy to say it that way? I mean, jeezes?"

I shrugged.

"I mean, he's got a lot to look after. He's supposed to hear our prayers and grant our wishes like a host on one of those miracle make-over television programs where the disabled kid suddenly gets the room of her dreams all because someone decided to grant a wish. I've heard those kids holler, 'thank you, Jesus!'"

I couldn't argue with that. What she was saying did not make theological sense but it made human sense.

"So, good things happen because something goes right, somewhere in the universe. That's a good thing, right? If someone is here to save the world, saying his name out of a sense of wonder or frustration or a search for clarity, isn't blasphemy. It's an expression of something that's gone right. Human beings can't be perfect. That's why we got Jesus in the first place. He was supposed to show us how to be human by trying to be perfect and failing at it." I couldn't say that around the house but I could tell my sister.

Jesus was everywhere when we were growing up.

We weren't churchy people, I heard my Mom say once. There was a family of churchy people down the block, really strict parents whose kids never smiled. They were heavily into Jesus but not into the happiness that comes when a wish gets granted. They said that because we were Anglicans, sometimes, we weren't Christian. That irked the bejeezus out of me. I had a right to say I was Christian and not because some kid down the block said I was or wasn't.

But those kids, we learned later, were 'born-agains.'

There is nothing wrong with born-agains, I suppose. My Mom told me I was a 'difficult birth,' that I came out with the cord wrapped around my neck, which is supposed to be lucky. I'm lucky I didn't die, I guess. Mom said she said a prayer of thanks to Jesus. But, thanks, being born once was probably tough enough and I'd hate to do it a second time with something choking me and cutting my odds of survival.

That was a topic one day when my sister and I were teenagers and we were sitting around in the rec room. Everyone has to find 'recreation' or 're-creation' of some kind, and if not in a badly panelled basement then in some sort of soulful satisfaction. We were sitting around talking about what we'd do if we could remake the world as in 're-creation.'

I'm not against people believing what they want. I don't like it when people start telling others what to believe. People should mind their own business.

But the strictness of those kids bothered me. The sneering down their noses with an 'our-shit-don't-stink' attitude got under my skin. I suppose I could have felt *schadenfreude* when, about ten years later, I heard the eldest kid, a boy whose stringy blond hair he grew longer and longer over his eyes until you couldn't see what he was thinking, showed up on his parents' doorstep with a ten gauge shotgun and blew his parents' heads off. Then killed his youngest sister. I mean, what did the youngest sister do, other than be obedient because she didn't know anything other than what she'd been told—what did she do? My sister told me what had happened. You can guess what I said, and I couldn't help feeling that the churchy family had betrayed their own best hopes. Assigning blame is pointless and judging people's behaviour is even worse, but why did he have to do that to his family?

Families are supposed to get on each others' nerves. That's the reason for having a family. If you are close to your family you can approach the junk in life with more calm. Things don't ruffle you as much. You've lived your life defending your little patch one minute and forgiving the attacker the next. That's what respect is: the right to be angry slowly and forgive instantly.

Our churchy moment came once each year. It was Easter. We were supposed to be sad for Jesus. We had an old hi-fi in our rec room and we played our records on it. My sister and

I were feeling sad one Easter—sad not only for Jesus but because it was a beautiful, warm, spring day and we were told to lay low in the rec room. To cheer ourselves up, we decided to hear some music. And we turned it up. Mom was upstairs making dinner and she seemed sad, too. She came bombing down the stairs and grabbed *Abbey Road* off the turn table. She threated to snap it over her knee if we played it again that Easter weekend.

"Show some respect," she said. "Here Comes the Sun" wasn't working for her.

We wanted her to listen. We wanted her to hear that Easter is a time when everyone emerges, either from their lost, lonely selves, from teenagerhood to adulthood or from awkward youth to the first thrill of discovery. Everything is bright and beautiful. Everything is worth singing about. When I hear that song, I think of George Harrison, his marriage on the rocks, his head all messed up with trying to find the world by running away from it to a mountain-side in India, only to arrive back in the Western world and find it just as much of a strict mess as it always has been, a world wanting to believe in something and grasping for a materialism that is unattainable, and then sitting down in Eric Clapton's garden and strumming on a guitar—that was re-creation.

The sun comes out.

Growing up was a long, cold, lonely winter, but there was always hope for us. There is always that remote possibility built into our inner lives of seeing around the edges of death. *Here comes the sun, and I say it's all right.*

A few months ago, my sister and I were talking during one of our late night phone conversations. The phone is our rec room replacement. She lives on the other coast. I'm still close to home. We were catching up on the news of the old neighbourhood. She'd forgotten that the family down the block that never smiled had been slaughtered. "When was that again?" she asked. As you get older, time means less because you aren't being reminded of it by a parent or a teacher. Instead the tables are turned and it is you who does the reminding of others.

"About ten years ago," I said, because I measure time in decades so there doesn't seem as much of it now.

"I was thinking of them the other day," my sister said, "and caught myself saying 'Jesus' because I could never figure them out. For a moment I thought it was funny, and then I felt badly. They were so into Jesus they strangled on the idea of him. Now, I think: 'Jesus, what were they thinking?'"

I wanted to laugh, too, and told her I wanted to laugh, but it would probably be in bad taste. Then I reminded her of the bully across the street, a fat kid with no forehead who went around punching people and sitting on them whenever he felt like it. It had been a welcome day when he moved away. I had been delivered from my enemy. My prayers had been answered by Jesus.

Our mother told me not to hit him back. "He has problems," she said. I think I screamed at her saying something like: "Yeah? Jesus! I got a problem, too. I'm the one getting beaten up!" A few minutes later I told her I was sorry I'd yelled at her.

The bully didn't get it when I wouldn't fight back. He just kept flailing away until my nose bled. Blood frightened him so he would get up and run home and tell his mother I had attacked him with a stick. He was the definition of a suck. I, on the other hand, was just trying to live up to what I was told to do. I had turned the other cheek and was as bruised as the first one he pounded. But I'd lie on the ground and take it. I'd think: "Why doesn't Jesus appear and help me?"

I guess Jesus works in mysterious ways. The bully's father, who sat in his rec room every night and every day of the weekend and vacations and holidays and put back bottle after bottle of rye, drove his car into a restaurant and died in the process of killing two people. So, "where was Jesus?" I asked. Jesus came in a moving van and took the bully and all his stuff away. I saw him. Jesus had long hair and a beard and could lift an entire dresser in his bare hands. Then I felt a horrible sense of guilt. Had my prayer been answered by those people who died? I mean, they were just sitting there, eating their dinner, and the guy drove a car at them.

"In retrospect," I told my sister, "I am sorry I prayed for deliverance."

"You had every right. And besides, Jesus doesn't turn people into alcoholics, or at least he's not supposed to, just so some kid on the other side of the street doesn't get sat on and punched in the face. And he didn't tell the dumb kid's father to take two people with him when he took his own life. There's no causality except in what you do to be a good person and not do crap to others. Jesus's literature says so."

But I'm troubled. Deep inside, I can't be happy with myself because of what I have been taught to believe, namely that I have to live with things I don't want to happen to me. Something has to die for something else to live. That's what the Roman philosopher Propertius said. "The death of one thing is the life of something else." The idea that what we wish for can come true is awful because something else has to suffer for it. Maybe that's the way of the world but I don't like it. Why couldn't people just change? Why couldn't some light, like something in a movie, come through a window while a choir utters a beautiful harmonic "aww" and a person could be changed for the better, transformed, transfigured, or just adjusted so people don't have to suffer because of them?

I made a mental note that, when I talked to my sister the next time, probably in a day or so, I'd ask her about a conversation in the recreation room at home—that a person dies many times in their life before they understand what they need to do to live in a way they can live happily with others. Those deaths, maybe spiritual deaths or just spurts of growth, doesn't make cowards of them, as Julius Caesar claimed, or at least as Shakespeare claimed on behalf of Caesar, but that the loss of what a person thinks he is or ought to be means a person can begin to be something new, something different, and with a little luck, something better.

THE BEGINNING

Ear to the Ground

A SPUR LINE ran near our town, though not through it. When the tracks were clear as far as we could see, we'd lay our heads on the rails, hear the hum and the vibration of the steel against the iron pins a gang of navvies had driven through the forests a century earlier, and guess how far the next freight might be. Sometimes, when there were no trains to be seen for miles in either direction, we could still tell that one was coming by feeling a distant vibration against our cheeks.

At night we heard the sound of the steel wheels on the tracks, the clack and shuttle of the box cars, and the wail of the horn at the level crossing. The line ran straight and even where it crossed the river on a low trestle bridge, then disappeared into the overgrowth of trees beyond where the eye could see.

My grandparents and parents had made promise pennies, laying them on the rails so that the wheels would roll over them and press them flat, the head of the king elongated and barely visible and the maple leaves on the back of the coin pulled sideways into dateless spans as if they spread in the full summer sun and made a cool shady place beneath their boughs.

Our parents could always tell when we'd been fooling around near the tracks. If we lay down, we picked up stains. Maybe it was the tell-tale creosote on our ear lobes, or just being out of ear shot when the late afternoon freight came through and we didn't hear our mothers calling us to supper. We were scolded about going near the tracks. We were threatened that we would be hit by a locomotive or crushed under the weight of the surging boxcar. If the engineer saw us from a distance, he would give us away by sounding his horn so that our parents knew, from the repeated wails that we had strayed from the woods, that we were playing with danger.

But if we timed it right, we could dash out of the trees without being seen and watch the boxcars roll by and feel the earth shaking beneath our feet. My grandfather had told me that, in the old days, the boys from the town would walk the tracks and pick up lumps of coal that had fallen from the scuttle car. The mill had closed and his father was running out of money. Just by walking the line from the town limits to the other side of the crossing, my grandfather collected enough coal to keep the stove in the kitchen fired until late November.

Crossing the tracks was against all the rules. The world that lay on the other side, the large, broad, undiscovered mystery we all wanted to possess someday, was a realm we could not enter, a promised land we could only see from a distance. It dawned on us that what lay beyond the tracks was the right side of life and we were all somehow on the wrong side. That made us wonder what our parents were keeping from us.

People left and never returned. The town was dying. So were many of the people in the town.

I sat with my grandfather in his room during the final,

long, hot summer of his life. He wouldn't say much, even when I asked him. He would stare out the window at the trees.

One day I asked him what the world was like. He'd left the town and come back. He'd seen the world, part of the time in khaki with a rucksack and rifle over his shoulder, and the other times with a briefcase of wares someone wanted him to sell.

He said there was a lot out there, more out there than I could imagine. It was not just geography or places on maps, he said, but the people, the ways they lived and spoke, the things they did that meant being on our side of the tracks contained an element of familiarity, a safety, a distance from the bad things that living on our side helped to keep in perspective.

By late August, his condition worsened. My grandmother said she couldn't look after him anymore. He was too demanding. My parents said it would break their hearts to tell him he would have to leave his house, his view from that upstairs window, and his town—the only things he could still call his own.

They came to me, the three of them—father, mother, grandmother. They told me it would be my duty to go with him by ambulance to the hospital in the city. They could make him comfortable there.

I shook my head. I could not betray him. It would tear his heart out to leave. He deserved to die in his town. He'd been faithful to the place when he could have gone anywhere in the world. He was the prodigal.

Couldn't they make him comfortable where he was?

No, they said. He would suffer more than he already had.

When the ambulance arrived, they loaded him in, and

he asked the orderlies when he'd be back home. He thought he was going away for a short stay. I got into the white Cadillac and sat squeezed up against the window.

I held his hand. I hadn't held it since I was a child, even though I was little more than a child the day they took him away. He must have known there was a point of no return, and he was headed toward it.

At the level crossing, the gate was up, and when we bumped over the rails, riding across the wooden floor of the road bed, I heard the wheels of the vehicle landing on the pavement where asphalt resumed. The old man snapped his hand away from mine.

I wanted to say something, but he turned his face and looked the other way. He could have looked back as the crossing disappeared and the road bent toward the city, but he did not; and he did not see me fighting to hold back the tears as I clutched a promise penny he'd given me in my left palm, the elongated sharp edge eating into my grasp.

The Higgins

THERE WERE LIMITS, always limits, but during his tenth summer, his limits grew broader and broader. Two blocks had been his range in the spring when he pointed out to his parents that his old bicycle with its tiny wheels was too small for him. Bigger wheels would mean more freedom. His urgency to discover the wider world was even more important because he was the new boy in school.

After moving to the neighbourhood, he'd met new friends —discovered courtesy of a pair of walkie-talkies his uncle gave him for his birthday that spring—and his world grew. When he broadcast as "The Red Fox," other boys in the area picked up his signal on their handsets and they agreed to rendezvous, just like commandos or secret agents. He held off meeting the other boys. He listened to their chatter on the airwaves. They were asking for him, but he knew they would mock his tiny bicycle. He had seen the other boys ride past his house. They had real bikes with plastic carriers on the front and hockey cards clothespinned to the wheel shafts so the spokes made the sound of an engine.

One day his father asked for a hand with something in the trunk of the family Ford. When the lid went up, there was a new bicycle, a red J.C. Higgins. Most of the boys had CCMs, but the Higgins, British-made, were heavier and sturdier. They could take a lot of wear. And the paint never seemed to chip on them even after several years. The boy was delighted.

His father warned him that there were still limits but in his daydreams, or before he fell asleep, or when he was in school listening to the teacher explain long division, or when he was supposed to be eating his dinner, all he could think about was the Higgins. He went to the rendezvous as an equal.

The other boys had spoken about the valley. It was ten blocks away, a steep ravine with a creek running through it. The boys said the creek bottom was a grey clay and if he wanted to make an ashtray for an aunt or uncle who smoked, all he had to do was dig it out of the bottom of the stream, shape it, and leave it to bake for a few hours in the heat of the summer sun.

When school finished, the boys decided to take on the valley. The ride was long and tedious. Suburban streets all look the same, and the boy wondered if he would be able to find his way home. When they arrived, they had to wheel their bikes down the incline. There was a path they could ride at the bottom, but the hill was known as Suicide Run. One of the boys' brothers had broken his arm trying to go down it while popping a wheelie on a dare.

When they reached the stream, they rolled up their jeans and waded in. The grey clay squished between his toes, and he scooped up a handful and found a good, flat, sun-beaten rock on which to work his ashtray. When he and the other boys were finished, they lay on the bank. One of them remarked that this was living, and the boy wondered why such a beautiful part of life had been off-limits to him for so long.

They left their bikes in the riverbank scrub and went up the path to explore. In the bushes, they heard a man muttering to himself. The man's clothes were dirty and tattered. His face was covered in a stubble of beard, and beside him lay three empty bottles, a plastic bag, and a crushed tube of model airplane glue like the one the boy used to build his planes and ships. The words "Use sparingly" popped into his mind. The man was naked from the waist down. His hand was stroking his groin and he was singing a song about a woman that the boys hadn't heard before.

The man turned and saw them. He jumped up and his wiener was erect in his hand. The man bent down and grabbed one of the empty bottles and threw it at the boy, but he ducked. Instead it hit one of his friends and opened a gash on the friend's forehead. With one boy bleeding, the others ran. The injured friend writhed on the ground and the man ran at him.

The boy realized he could not leave his friend behind. He called out to the others. They had to save their fallen friend. They regrouped and ran back, each of them picking up sticks and stones on the way. The man had their bleeding friend by the arm and was shaking him and pulling at the injured boy's trousers. The boy was screaming: "Leave me alone!" Then, they all attacked.

One of the stones hit the man in the eye. That was a good shot, someone said. The man let go of the bleeding boy and the young gang ran as hard as they could. When they reached their bicycles, they grabbed them and ran back up the hill except for the bleeding boy. He had to leave his bike behind.

At the top of the valley, the boy told his injured friend to hop on the seat, and he pedalled as hard as he could on his

Higgins all the way to the friend's house. The friend's mother was gardening and looked up as the posse arrived. The boy had his friend's blood all over the back his shirt. The mother, without waiting to hear the story of how the friend had been injured, pulled out her car keys from her pocket and drove her bleeding son away at high speed.

That night, the boy's father appeared just before bedtime on the front porch with a group of his friend's fathers around him. He had a lock in one hand and the smashed CCM of his injured friend in the other.

"You must never go back to the valley. There are buggers down there. One won't be bothering anyone for a long time but buggers nonetheless. I'm locking up your bike for a week to teach you that there are places you can go and places you can't go."

The world grew smaller from that night on.

The boy lay in the dark, thinking about the man and what could have dragged him down to the valley.

He thought about the scar on his friend's head, and how he would always wear it on the outside, and perhaps on the inside.

He didn't understand why the man hurt so much that he would want to hurt any of them.

As he lay awake, anticipating the long ride in the other direction to junior high in September and perhaps starting a delivery service for some of the local stores with his Higgins, he concluded that freedom was not what he thought it was; that the world was a small and troubled place; and that his Higgins would only take him so far.

Knowledge

IT WAS DARK inside the cat, but the bird wouldn't know that anymore. The mother robin was frantic, but as birds probably do, she would soon forget what happened—the hatchlings pale and veiny lay scattered around the base of the apple tree and the spattering of her mate's blood dripped from the boughs and branches. She'd find a new mate just as red and just as capable if not better at making a nest. The problem wasn't the birds or the cat. It was Joey.

Joey had to spend April, May, and early June in his room. He had to sleep when he felt tired. His glands were swollen, and the doctor told him if he ever wanted to have children he had to take it easy. His dishes and cutlery needed to be boiled. He couldn't touch the taps in the bathroom with his hands. His father duct-taped six-inch rulers to the faucets, so Joey could turn them on and off with his elbows. And maybe if he didn't have to turn the taps on and off he'd have the energy to have children when he grew up.

Little things. That's what makes illness less contagious. And learning how to cope, how to deal with the bad things, his mother had told him, things that are here to test us so that we know what is true and what is false, and what is worthy of our love and demanding of our fears.

The birds, Joey thought, were worthy of his love. They became his pastime. He could see them through his window when he lay in bed. First the father bird hopped on the back of the mother bird. He couldn't see the details, but they were mating or as the guys at school called it, fucking. He wondered why people said fuck when they were surprised by something or angry at someone. Hopping on the back of something didn't involve either surprise or anger for the birds, as far as he could see.

Then the robins built a nest together. Joey's father called that the long haul. Joey wasn't sure what the long haul was either. "He's in it for the long haul, son." The nest wasn't going anywhere.

Joey's mother put out wool as the father bird, the one with the redder chest, who wove twigs together as if he had found the plans in *Popular Mechanics,* the one magazine of his father's Joey was permitted to read. The mother bird laid eggs. Joey thought that's what the guys at school meant when they talked about someone getting laid. Each one was slightly speckled, robin's egg blue eggs, because robins lay blue eggs and the colour is named after them.

One morning when the sun came through the branches of trees, the eggs cracked and alien-like creatures, naked, beaked, big-eyed, veiny, lay in the nest with the mother robin on top of them just as she had sat on top of the eggs after she laid them.

He'd written to his science teacher that he didn't have a microscope at home and the school refused to lend him one, so he couldn't see the paramecium like the other kids. He told the science teacher about the birds.

"Okay," the teacher wrote back. "Your project is to record what the birds do each day as they go from eggs to hatchlings to pin-feathered nestlings. You are going to be the class ornithologist." Joey thought the word sounded cool. He said it to himself several times until it tripped off his tongue. "Record every detail until their mother pushes them out of the nest and they fly away."

Joey hadn't counted on the cat. It was not the neighbour's cat. The McGowans next door kept their cat on a short chain in their backyard. They said it was to keep it from spraying. Joey thought spraying meant it peed on things, but his older brother said that spraying was a cat's way of getting off. Joey wasn't sure what his brother meant.

There had to be plausibility in what his brother said. Joey asked his mother if there was.

"Your father will have to have *the talk* with you about the birds and the bees."

Joey was confused. Robins build a nest. Robins come out of eggs. What did bees have to do with it? He knew bees pollinated things. Did they pollinate eggs? Were eggs like flowers? If baby birds lived long enough, were they fed honey? Was that it? His science teacher would need a report from Joey so Joey wouldn't fail Grade Five. Mono was not a good reason for failing Grade Five. If he was older, mono was an excuse for all sorts of things. His brother stopped dating a girl he didn't like in Grade Eight and to make her go away he told her *he* had mono.

The cat climbed the apple tree. The father robin tried to protect the babies. Joey thought the word was in-sync. The father bird was just showing his in-syncs. The bird had lunged at the cat, dug its claws in the cat's hackles that were up because the cat not only had to attack the nest but had to give the appearance of attacking the nest as if it meant business.

Joey had seen the back hairs stand up on his grandmother's German shepherd before the dog died of old age, and his grandmother said: "It has its hackles up because it sees a cat." Cats probably had hackles too because they had fur on their backs.

The cat pawed at the air and the father robin got too close to peck it and got pinned against an upright branch. That's when the cat bit the bird's head off. The father robin's wings flapped furiously but without a head it didn't know when to stop and it fell from the tree without flying. Then the cat started inching toward the nest.

"No! No!" Joey shouted and banged on the glass, but the cat looked at him as if it didn't care. It just looked at him as if he wasn't there. Joey yelled: "Fucking cat!" But realized that fucking was probably something else and he felt horribly tired, exhausted, and angry, and was afraid his mother had heard him using a swear word.

The mother robin was making weird sounds in her throat, not song but screeching as if she was terrified or pissed off. She flew to one of the higher branches where the cat could not come after her. Then the nest got knocked off the bough by the cat and the baby birds fell and bounced off the exposed roots of the apple tree.

Joey could see them on the grass below his window. The cat climbed down, skidding part way where the trunk became straight up and down, digging in its claws and almost falling forward with anxiousness to reach the remains of the father bird. The cat tore open the body of the father bird and then shoved it aside when it did not want it anymore.

One of the hatchlings had landed on a lower branch, close enough to see through the window, and was raising its head though its eyes, round and dark blue under thin eyelids, could not open. Its head bobbled and wavered and fell back.

The round bulb of the body was pale, roundish flesh with veins he could see through the skin. As the cat climbed up the tree for a second time, it approached the hatchling that lay on its back on the branch. The small bird's belly rose and fell, and then it shuddered and was motionless. Joey recorded the incident in as much detail as he could write. He was driven to tears by what he had seen and he thought the only way he could do justice for the robins was to be their ornithologist.

Joey's teacher phoned his mother several days later. Joey heard his mother's half of the conversation from his room. It sounded as if the teacher was upset with what Joey had given him. Joey worried that he might have to repeat Grade Five. His father and mother came to his room and sat down on the edge of the bed.

"Are you confused, son?" his father asked.

"About what?"

"About the birds and the bees."

His mother said: "We think it is time we had *the talk* with you."

Joey felt embarrassed but he was not sure why. He felt as if something, maybe his confusion, maybe his understanding of how he thought things worked, maybe the fabric of the world he trusted and had always known was about to be taken from him. He was afraid of what they would tell him. His father sat and stared at the science report Joey had written about the robins.

Joey wrote that the cat next-door sprayed and wasn't to blame, and how the fucking birds took twigs and wool and patched things up between them, and how the hatchlings looked like his eye ball or his private parts, and how life was about misery, about getting his head bitten off, about sleeping all day because he could not stay awake if he wanted to have children, and how the father robin must have been sleeping when the cat climbed the tree because he wanted to have more baby birds and needed his rest. Joey wrote that, when he went to sleep at night, he did not see girls or mother robins even though both were not there and he never bothered to think about them so he wouldn't spray like the neighbour's cat, but only saw darkness when he closed his eyes except for when he dreamed.

When he dreamed, he saw the sight and sound of a helpless baby bird being chewed in a cat's mouth, a cat he had never seen before and that probably didn't live in the neighbourhood, ruining his science project so he would have to repeat Grade Five, not because he was stupid but because he had to sleep all day and all night and only opened his eyes to see how the birds were doing and wonder why they were doing it.

He explained that the robins built a nest with wool his mother had set in the lower branches of the apple tree, and that when the nest fell from its cradle in the branches a single strand of red Phentex was still attached to the bough and it dangled alone in the breeze, and the cat that had killed the birds lay in the branch where the nest had been and batted the skein like a toy as it moved back and forth with the wind.

And if he could have children someday, if he ever recovered and was able to stay awake, he was afraid of being devoured by something he could not even see because his eyes were too young to open even if he could lean against the window frame with the sash raised now the warm weather was here and listen for the buzzing of bees among the fingerling twigs and nodes that wanted to bear apples but had to be awakened for them to grow.

Constant

MY SISTER SAID God had nothing to do with it, that our father was to blame. I should have killed the old man but decided he wasn't worth the bother. If I had, God would have wanted me dead, and killing God, my sister said, was next to impossible.

Every Sunday morning before the sun came up, our father would rouse the four of us from our warm beds and set us to work around the house. We could have understood getting up that early on that day if we had embraced religion with specified times to pray. At least we would have made God happy. But our father was adamant that spiritual beliefs were fallacies. He had a long argument about why people believe things and why we shouldn't, and in the midst of his knotted logic we were on the receiving end of both our old man and the Almighty. The only thing we had to cling to, deep down inside, was that we all had to be busy or we were lazy good-for-nothings. The more tired and exhausted we became, the more our father said we weren't believing in him.

Mom had always kept the place spic and span, but after she passed—I was the youngest and was ten at the time—there was no stopping our father from taking up the theology of cleanliness. He would rant that his wife had been the patron saint of sparkling.

The bathroom and kitchen faucets had to shine. Not a footprint could be seen on the living room carpet. No one ever went in there. Our only tv was in the corner so if we wanted to watch anything we had to sneak off to a friend's place, and if our father found us missing there was hell to pay. My sister always vacuumed her way out.

We learned a kind of sanitation art, how to do things in such a way as to magnify our work in his eyes. If we gave a window an extra polish with a soft cloth it would shine and reflect his face, and he loved to see his face in the glass with the outside overlaid on it. He said it made him feel part of the world.

My two older brothers figured out how to hide nicks and scratches in the furniture with the sweat and grease that beaded on their faces. We did everything to please our father. None of that mattered.

One by one, my older siblings fled. My sister was the last to go and she left me alone. I thought that was crappy. She held up her hands one Sunday afternoon. Her cuticles were bleeding from the cleanser, the bleach having eaten away the natural luster of her nails. She slapped our father's face and left an imprint of her blood on his cheeks.

When I was sixteen, I got a job working for a shipping company down by the lakeshore. I told the old man I was getting a job, that I wasn't a lazy good-for-nothing, and he said he was going to take ninety percent of each paycheque as compensation for the work my brothers and sister had put him to. I agreed. I wasn't up for a fight. I'd make the money go where I wanted it to go.

Emptying or loading a transport was a night's work, and the pay was good. I was saving up to get away from the bastard. I had no intention of just walking out. I wanted to land on my feet. My second-oldest brother had just left with nothing to go to. He got into drugs. I don't know where he found the money. The only thing he knew how to do was clean. The rest of his short life was a mess. When they found his body in an alley, all my father could say was that my brother died in filth.

The Sunday of my departure came when I was so bone weary I couldn't move my arms. The night before, with a push on to empty three trucks rather than the usual one and turn around a shipment in record time—I imagined a man from the *Guinness Book* standing behind the plastic drape on the loading dock with a stopwatch and a clipboard—I wasn't sure where I was let alone whether I had broken any records. Our foreman was just as bad as my Dad. He kept me late, long after the buses stopped running, and I had walked home the six miles as dawn was coming up only to be awakened twenty minutes after I got in to "put my nose to the grindstone."

My father's wake-up calls were coming earlier and earlier because he had stopped sleeping. When I heard his voice telling me to get up and get to it I told him to fuck off. He disappeared and came back with a bucket of kitchen compost and dumped it in my bed.

"Look at the rot you live in," he yelled.

I got up, showered, shaved, and packed my bags. I had some friends from work who told me if I ever needed to I could crash on their couch. I did. I slept on that couch until I finished my final high school term. My father would appear on Saturday nights and yell at me on the loading dock until the foreman got tired of him coming up and interrupting the rhythm of our work and had him arrested for trespassing.

My sister moved back to the city. Her venture out west didn't work out. They guy she hooked up with, she said, was just as crazy as our father. She had done okay on her return, got a nice apartment, bought a car, and cleaned up her act, as she put it wryly. She took me in. She said that without the bother of a boyfriend nagging her to do this or that, it would be good to have me around. I think she was afraid our father was going to come for her. I was her protection.

One summer evening we drove by the old house. It was for sale. We stopped and asked one of the neighbors what had happened to our old man.

"You didn't hear? He spent all his time cleaning. We saw him scrubbing the driveway. He was down on his hands and his knees. We pretended not to notice because if people want to do weird shit, well, they have a right, and who are we to question. But we should have questioned. The hazmat people had to evacuate half the block. Your Dad decided to concoct the perfect toilet bowl cleaner. He'd said something like that to Harry next door, and Harry told him to be careful. Your old man almost killed us. He'd left the window open and green clouds of mustard gas poured out and rolled down the street. A couple of boys who were playing road hockey had to be hospitalized. The old guy had mixed bleach, vinegar, and toilet-bowl cleaner in a bucket. He'd made about five, maybe six gallons of the stuff before it got to him. He'd set the buckets in each room. Maybe he thought he was going to let the gas clean the walls. Who knows? By the time we found him the paint was peeling off the walls and he had drowned in his own lungs."

My sister and I wanted to cry all the way back to her place. We had a right to cry. We couldn't. Our father had been the one constant in our lives, and he was gone. But after a long silence as we turned on to the lakeshore expressway to head back to the comfortable mess my sister lived in and in which I was now a part, a bug spattered on the windshield and out of habit, I opened the car window, leaned almost entirely out and began to try to rub it clean with my sleeve. I felt guilty, not for the bug, but for the mess.

She pulled me back inside the car, asked me what on earth I was thinking. I didn't know. I looked at her and tried to explain the smudge that was now spread across the sleeve of my shirt. She looked at me in shock for a moment, and we both began to cry.

"We need to make a clean break from the past," she said, and realizing her words cut both ways, she pulled into an empty parking lot and shut off the car. We looked at each other through salt tears that tried to cleanse our eyes but they only stung us deeply so neither of us could see where we'd ended up.

Monster

HE GROWLED WITH every spade of the front yard flower bed he turned over. His brows were heavy beneath a floppy black newsboy cap that was worn to threads around the edge of the peak. He dressed in cheap, black canvas work clothes of the kind the hostels gave to men who needed to prove their way in the world through the sweat of hard work, and he squinted when he stood up and the sun traced the lines on his sunken cheeks. His shoulders were more than a yard across. Boar-bristle hairs protruded from his ears. He could have been a child's idea of Frankenstein's monster had he not rolled his own cigarettes and sat and smoked them on the edge of the street gutter when he took a break for a few minutes after every three hours of work.

The kids on the block taunted him. They called him 'Monster.' When he bent over, they threw pebbles at his back. Jacob saw it happen. The man didn't deserve that. His feet were swollen, and their tops almost protruded through the laces. The man was not well, but said he needed the work.

"I'd put him in his late seventies," Jacob's grandfather said. "He's odd. Sometimes if I ask him a question, he just turns away. He doesn't trust anyone. I've asked him about his past and he never answers. He's a bit like an animal who was beaten too often."

"I asked him a question," Jacob said as they sat eating their lunch. Jacob's grandfather had fallen on a rickety escalator, the oldest in the city, and the resulting back injury had left him unable to tend his garden. "His name is Lawrence and, if you call him sir, he will talk to you. He likes tea. I asked him. He said he likes it in a good china cup. I want to bring him some."

"Not in my good china, you won't," his grandmother said. "He's an itinerant. You don't know what a man like that might do, and we know nothing about him."

Lawrence spoke with a heavy working-class English accent. Jacob's grandmother surmised the labourer may have been a Bernardo boy from the Midlands, Manchester possibly, a child of the Victorian slums who had been scooped up and brought Canada. "There were such terrible slums in that city." The Bernardo children had been taken away from their families. The boys, especially the boys, would turn to crime if they grew up poor in England. Most were nothing more than cheap, child-labour, and when they suffered and broke under their masters, they were buried in a farm's back-forty, or worse, fed to the hogs. Jacob wondered what it was like to be homeless. The family barber his grandfather, father, and Jacob visited every two weeks had been one of the "rescued" slum boys. He'd run away from a farm and done errands in Toronto until he saved enough money to go to barber school. Lawrence hadn't been that lucky. Fred the barber was part of the community. Lawrence was living at the Sally Ann.

"Can't we ask him in for tea?" Jacob asked.

"He's a labourer who came to the door looking for work one day. We can't ask him in," the grandmother said. "We don't know who he is. I agree with your grandfather. Lawrence is an odd chap. He's had a hard life but I don't want to know about it."

"He's been all right," the grandfather said. "Since my fall, Lawrence has done all right for us. He works hard. He never complains. I think we can ask him in."

The labourer sat at the kitchen table. Jacob's grandmother laid a plate of sandwiches before the man, some egg, others ham, and set a pot of tea on the enamel topped table and stepped back to watch from the other side of the kitchen. Lawrence blinked as if stunned and then squinted. The sandwiches disappeared two at a time. Lawrence looked at the tea pot. "May I have it in a cup? I haven't had tea in a proper cup in years." Jacob's grandmother poured the tea into an old metal measuring cup. He stretched out his feet so one leg protruded beyond the table and bent over and rubbed his ankle. He winced.

Jacob asked Lawrence why his feet were swollen.

"Ay? My feet are bad. They've never been good. Wish I didn't have them, but I need them," he replied and shoved the remaining quarter sandwiches in his mouth and washed them down with a single gulp of a cup. He leaned across the table and poured himself more tea as Jacob's grandmother stood against the sink and wiped her hands on her apron.

When the tea and sandwiches were gone, Lawrence went back to digging. As the blade delved down in the ground, the labourer turned over the shovel and groaned. Jacob's grandmother set off with her bundle-buggy behind her to do some shopping on the main street. Jacob's grandfather went upstairs to have a nap on the daybed of the study. Jacob leaned against the window frame in the dining room and watched Lawrence who was in the backyard now, turning over clods of mud, bending to pull weeds, and growling whenever he stood up.

Jacob went to the back door, stopping in the kitchen to haul a cauldron out from the lower cupboard where his grandmother kept her heavy canning pots, then filled the cauldron, put it on the stove, and after a few minutes, before it became too hot, the boy opened the back door and set the cauldron at the foot of the porch.

"Lawrence, I have something to help your feet." Lawrence stood up, drove his spade into the flower bed, put his hand to the small of his back, and squinted. "Come here. This will help."

The labourer shuffled across the garden and sat down on the second step from the bottom of the back porch.

"Take off your shoes and socks and soak your feet for a moment." The Englishman looked confused, then nodded and undid his shoelaces. The feet did not want to come away easily, and Jacob had to tug to free the left, then the right shoes. The socks were rank. The sharp odour stung Jacob's nose. "When was the last time you changed your socks, sir?"

"Can't recall."

They stared at the man's feet. As the socks came off, so did layers of skin. The nails were long and green. He had the feet of a monster. Jacob noticed the man's fingernails. They were green and brown and long as well. Maybe the kids from down the block were right.

"Put them in the cauldron quick," Jacob said. "Does that feel better?"

Lawrence nodded. The socks smelled of decay. "Lawrence? You can't wear those socks. They're awful."

"All I have."

"I'm going to take them and bury them in the garden. My grandfather has a pair of green argyles. He never wears them. He said he wouldn't be caught dead in green argyles. Do you mind if your socks are green?"

The labourer looked at Jacob and squinted as if he didn't understand.

"I'll get you new socks." The boy went up to his grandfather's room, opened the sock drawer of the *haute bois*, and pulled out a paddy green pair of argyles that had been gathered into a ball. They smelled of sweet cedar. As he passed the linen closet in the upper hall, he found the oldest, rattiest, towel in the cupboard, and brought it downstairs with him.

"Dry your feet now, Lawrence, and put on these socks." Lawrence held up the socks and smiled. Jacob fetched the shovel and carried the old socks to the back of the garden where he dug a hole and dropped them in before turning the soil on top of them. By the time he returned, Lawrence had dried his feet, and had his feet in the socks. "Are they pinching?" Jacob asked as he did up Lawrence's laces. The man shook his head.

"The feet feel better," Lawrence said as if they were not his feet but someone else's. "Thank you."

The cauldron had cooled off. The surface was floating with bits of scum as the boy tilted the water onto the walkway and watched it flow into the grass.

Jacob's grandmother appeared on the porch. She stared at the boy and the man. "What are you doing?" she asked abruptly. "Aren't those my husband's socks?"

"Gran, I gave them to him. His feet were in awful shape. I washed his feet for him. He could hardly stand up."

The grandmother glared, not knowing what to make of the situation. "What made you do such a thing? And you, what made you sit there and let my grandson do that for you?"

Lawrence squinted up at the woman. He reached down as if he was about to remove the socks and give them back to her. "They don't match me trousers," he said.

"Please, let him keep them, Gran. Grampa doesn't wear them. He told me how much he dislikes argyles. Lawrence needs them, and I buried his old ones because his feet were still partly in them and they smelled worse than death."

As she turned to head back up the steps into the kitchen, the woman paused, looked at her grandson, and shook her head. "Charity begins at home, and I guess you think you live here," she said, looking at the boy. "As for you, Lawrence, get back to work. I'll put the kettle on for a fresh pot of tea."

Sadness

KING SAID NOTHING should have that look of sadness in its eyes, not a person nor an animal nor even knots in a pine board, but Billgo had it. He was staring straight ahead when we found him the next morning. He'd been standing at the freezer door, staring into the small rectangular window his breath had fogged over and covered in a jack-frost pattern of ice. It was a look that pleaded for an answer yet at the same time faced the truth of the situation. King said things should never look that sad, but I'd seen the look before when Billgo had me pull the noose around the necks of the cows we slaughtered in back before cutting them up and hanging them in the freezer. And it was my fault that Billgo was dead. I was the one who'd shut him in the cold, thinking he'd already gone home.

It was an accident and all, but I probably shouldn't have been working there. I was only fourteen and there are laws that say a fourteen-year-old shouldn't be working in an abattoir, home of the fresh-killed cutlet, but Billgo owed my father a favour or two and my old man decided he didn't want me sitting around the house all summer or getting up to no good behind other people's stores. I was brought into Barley's because Billgo told my dad I could learn a thing or two about life by being there. I had strong shoulders. I didn't have a strong spirit.

The first morning on the job, Billgo took me into the slaughter room, as he called it. There was a brown heifer there. Billgo said it had stopped milking and the best it could do for its owner was a quick turn-around to the table. The animal stood docile. It stank of barn and urine even after I washed it down. I wanted to speak to it, but when the first words left my lips, Billgo looked up from the grindstone where he was sharpening his knife and said: "No, no! It's all business here."

It was my job to hold the heifer's head still so Billgo could apply the bolt to kill the animal instantly. It was supposed to be humane for the animal. King was out front dealing with a restaurant owner who'd come by to hand-pick his steaks from the freezer and to dicker about the prices. King was good at dickering. I hadn't learned how to do that yet.

Billgo looped the noose around the heifer's neck and, after it was tightened, he told me on the count of three to pull hard. I made the mistake of looking in the cow's eyes. They were brown and round and trusting, yet they were sad. The creature knew that something was not right. Animals read people's feelings. My dog knows when I am sad, and since the morning when we did the heifer I haven't been able to play with Sandy, not like before, when I would throw her a stick and she'd retrieve it and we'd roll together on the grass and she'd look at me with her big round eyes that told me she loved me.

The heifer's eyes didn't say they loved me. They looked at me with a "what now?" expression, as if it wanted to know what would come next, as if I held the answer to what it would see or know or learn. And I wasn't strong enough. The rope noose merely irritated the creature and she bellowed a disgruntled groan, not a moo, but a moan and shook her head as the cold steel of the bolt machine touched the top of her head and snapped into work.

I wanted to cry. Billgo saw the look in my eyes and said: "Hey kid, this'll learn you life and make a man out of you." The cow's eyes stared in disbelief for an instant. I wanted to turn away, but I kept looking, kept wanting to give the beast an atom of love or reassurance or hope—and all hope fails in an abattoir—that the world was not a cold, indifferent place, that its life had been a life spent among all the things a beast might love—the suck of a calf at its teat, a new trough of fodder, the blinding sunlight of the yard and the pasture beyond as it stepped from the barn after a long cold night on the threshold of spring. Then its eye balls rolled, and its whites appeared like sunrise as it knelt before me, its front legs buckling, then its hind legs, and the lids fluttered as if it could not see and wanted to see as the sadness left it to look through the veil of a glassy stare.

I ran to the concrete sink and threw up. Billgo laughed. King stood in the door.

"Hey kid, it's like that," King said, slapping his hand on the doorframe. "This is what puts food on the table." Cold, indifferent, but true: This is what puts food on the table.

The chickens and turkeys I got used to. Billgo ordered me to come into the slaughterhouse every time he had a new arrival. And after the deed had been done, after King had raised the animal up on a hook and cut its length so the purple and pink and bloody entrails poured out, and after I had shovelled the unwanted parts into the steel hamper and hosed down the floor, I kept thinking of what I had just done and I felt a shame before the world that hung around me like a shadow.

By the end of the summer, I was praying every night that something might be different, that I might find a way out of the job that would not shame my father or tell Billgo and King I was afraid, or that I suffered a death inside me with every animal they brought down.

The last week in August came and I was thinking about going back to school, though I was uncertain if I could stay in school, if I could cut open a splayed frog on a wax-bedded tray or dissect an earthworm, let alone sit through conjugations of verbs, each one expanding its subjects until everyone was culpable of the action at its root. I probably wasn't paying attention when I thought I heard Billgo saying he was leaving early because it was his kid's birthday or that King said he'd lock up and told me to go to the back and shut down the freezer.

I wasn't aware that there was anyone in there when I turned off the light. I hadn't thought, as I usually did when asked to shut down the freezer, of bending down and looking under the sides or between the shelves where we kept the steaks and cutlets in boxes. It just didn't occur to me. I flipped the switch, closed the door behind me, and pushing the chrome lock handle into place, told King that the freezer was secured and followed him out the door as he turned to lock it.

Around midnight my father woke me and asked if Billgo had been down the day before. Usually when Billgo was feeling "under-the-weather," as he put it, he would go to the local bar, the Milepost, and put back a few. It wasn't like him to miss his kid's party, especially when he was bringing home the best steaks for the adults' barbecue. No one thought to look back at the shop. My old man and I drove up and down the streets, slowly, peering in every alley and doorway in case Billgo had fallen down drunk.

The next morning, I met King at the door of the shop. We stood for a couple of minutes, looked up and down the street, as if expecting Billgo to show up. Instead, King got out his key and went to turn the light on in the slaughterhouse while I was sent to open the freezer, and there was Billgo.

He was still wearing the chain mail glove on his left hand, the holding hand, and in his cutting hand were five large T-bones. He was staring straight at the window, patiently, as if he was certain someone was coming, as if he thought it was all a joke or a mistake—which it was—and that when the door opened he would fire whoever was standing on the other side. But as the hours passed, he must have realized that his patience was not going to be answered, and that his eyes were brown, and round, and sad, with crystals of ice around them, his cheeks pale, his mouth slightly open, and a look of realization on him for which I have never found an answer.

Racket

I WAS GIVEN an old Slazenger that had been my Dad's. When he was growing up in the Thirties, kids must have had arms of steel because the racket weighed about ten pounds out of the press. A racket had to have a press. The frame was made of wood and the pressure of the cat-gutting strings could cause a frame to warp with moisture or time. I caught hell from my Dad when he saw me strumming the strings like a guitar. I was never sure if the strings were made from real cats or not, but when I strummed them, they played a G. It would have been easier to play tennis with a guitar. Guitars are lighter. With the press, the racket weighed more than ten pounds. Tennis took a lot of effort for a kid. I begged for one of the new rackets, which were slightly lighter.

My father had been an athlete. Not just an athlete. He had been captain of his high school tennis team. He could return a volley like he wanted to kill the person on the receiving end of it. The first time we played tennis, I had to duck. He told me I was a coward. I tolerated that. Cowards don't die with a tennis ball between their eyes.

The day I gave up tennis and I put the Slazenger in its press and tucked it in the back of my closet was the day my arm almost had to be amputated. I'd gone up to the public courts in our local park with a school friend named Mark. Our mothers played tennis together.

He was no good either. If we were lucky, we'd toss the ball into the air and it would make contact with the picture-frame around the gutting, and the ball would drop dead at the net. Once, I started screaming with joy because I got the ball over to Mark's side of the court. Mark called me a suck. I was being a suck. On my next serve, I launched a toss into the air and wound up for my serve. The ball struck the tip of the racket and went off at a ninety-degree angle. It lodged at the base of the net in the next court.

There was an Englishman shouting his score out loud so everyone could hear it. He was playing a younger man and berating him for wearing black socks on a tennis court. I felt sorry for the younger man. He was getting beaten five ways from Sunday. The Englishman was rubbing it in. Hard. I stood there for about five minutes. Mark and I had only one ball. It was a bald, almost dark grey ball because it also doubled for our road hockey games in the winter. I pointed to the ball. The English guy ignored me. I stood there. Mark told me to go and get it. I didn't know what to do. I wasn't going to tolerate it.

When the English guy—and get this, he was in one of those creamy-coloured V-neck sweaters like boaters wear at Cambridge or cricket players wear at Lords and looked very English in his long white trousers—stepped back from the line and called the score of his game and where his game was in the match, I assumed he was taking a break. He was bouncing the ball on the ground over and over and not looking at his opponent who was bent over at the back line, looking nervous and anxious for his ordeal to end. So, I went over and got my ball. I held it up for Mark to see. Mark looked happy. We could get on with failing at tennis.

That's when the English guy spoke up.

"Little man!" he said, his voice sneering as if I was some sort of subspecies that not only had to be scolded but dismissed, "You must never, ever, run across someone else's court."

"I wanted my ball and you weren't going to get it," I said.

"How dare you be impertinent!" he shouted.

Mark said: "Let's go home. It's a public tennis court and the guy doesn't have any manners."

The Englishman followed me home.

That was creepy.

What was even creepier was that as soon as I had gone to my room to put the racket in the press, the doorbell rang. I heard my mother speaking loudly to someone. It had been the Englishman. He told my mother that I was a rude little urchin. I didn't know what an urchin was. I thought he was calling me a spiny sea-creature.

My mother stood in the door of my bedroom. "You need to learn some manners," she said. "I'm locking up your bike for a week."

It was a public court. The English guy had no sense of etiquette. If he was playing there, he was, more or less, a neighbour and he needed to be neighbourly. He should have returned my ball. I had to put up with the punishment. I had to walk to school for a week, even in the rain.

And it was raining on the first day I got my bike back. The ground in the schoolyard turned to mud. If we got muddy enough, we could be sent home to change clothes and we'd take our time doing it. The janitor didn't like us tracking in filth from outside. He'd holler at us and tell us we looked like we'd been down in the ground and good and buried and his classrooms, classrooms he had to clean, weren't for mucky mucks like us. I was never sure if the janitor was kidding, but we all agreed he wasn't a bad guy. He just didn't like mud in his halls.

The best way to get muddy was a piggy-back fight. I put Mark on my back. Another boy, large for his age, had Roy on his back. As we charged each other in a joust to see if we could lose our footing, Roy's toe came up and kicked me square in the left elbow. I immediately dropped Mark and rolled in the mud.

A teacher came up and hollered: "Get up out of there! You're getting muddy on purpose!" I pointed to my arm once the pile had cleared off. I undid my long-sleeve shirt and there was my elbow protruding through the skin. I was sent home, muddy and broken.

My mother drove me to the hospital. The first doctor in the emergency ward was the young guy who'd gotten the tar kicked out of him on the tennis court days earlier. He shook his head.

"It looks bad. I'll have to call a specialist."

I could tolerate the pain. I could tolerate the emergency ward and the young doctor who added I would probably need a cast.

Then the Englishman appeared. He looked at me. "Injured, are we?" he asked sarcastically.

I nodded.

I left the hospital with my bones stuffed back into my skin, three stitches for which I received no anaesthesia, and my arm wrapped tight in gauze and surgical tape. No cast. I thought I deserved a cast. My friends could have signed it. It would have been a badge of honour. I asked for one. The Englishman just sneered in my face.

At four in the morning, I couldn't feel my fingers. By dawn, my arm was in excruciating pain. My mother phoned our doctor who called back at eight. "Cut off the bandages right now. That doctor has tied the whole thing up so tight the kid is going to lose his arm."

We had a doctor who came to the house if we were really sick or in a lot of pain. He examined my arm. "What did you do to that guy to deserve this?" he asked, not expecting an answer.

"I retrieved my tennis ball," I said. I told him the story of the tennis game. There was a long conversation between our doctor and my mother in the hall.

When I went back to the hospital several weeks later to have my cast removed, I instructed the young emergency doctor to do his best to cut around the signatures, drawings, and wise-ass sayings my friends had written on the plaster. I'd even gotten a hockey player to sign it.

"Where's the English guy?" I asked. "He did up my arm too tight and my doctor says I almost lost it."

"The English guy? Oh, he's no longer with this hospital. Lucky for me, I can play tennis now with someone who won't turn the game into murder."

Providence

ST. BIDDULPH'S HAD been a new church when the streets of the surrounding community pushed into the fields of wildflowers at the edge of the city. The day it opened, the parishioners remarked what a beautiful place it was, how quiet it had been during prayers when a wild canary was heard singing its heart out in an elm that stood on the side lawn.

Then the city encroached. The church was almost downtown, the area around it not yet ready to be renovated or torn down for newer structures, and the silence that had been a holy spell in St. Biddulph's was lost in the growl of traffic. Despite the noise, St. Biddulph's was the last bastion of a good choir in a denomination that had long-since ceased to be a voice in the community.

Every Thursday night, Thomas would arrive in the annex chapel where the boy choristers practiced from five to six thirty, and every Thursday night he would be met by his grandfather who would walk him back to the house for dinner. Thomas's grandfather had been one of the original members of the congregation, and now, as the years carried away the fortunes of St. Biddulph's, he was one of the last of the original congregation. His grandfather's face was grey as the stone upon which he and his fellows had built their church. The old man was ill. And, by the time Thomas was ready to join the choristers, his grandfather had grown deaf.

The church had been sold to a developer—every patch of land in the parish was on the verge of becoming costly, and with no appreciable congregation, save for a handful of parents who sent their children to join the remnants of a once-acclaimed choir, the pews were mostly empty on Sunday mornings, and as the years passed, Thomas's family moved pew by pew closer to the altar and the pulpit. They said it was so the old man could hear, but moving forward meant they had climbed the ladder of the congregation even though there wasn't one now.

There was only a handful of senior choristers and a few boy choristers such as Thomas who were the descendants of the senior members, and most of the elders sang off-key as a homage to their advanced years. The local high school orchestra agreed to accompany the choir on Easter Sunday for one last attempt at the *Hallelujah Chorus* before the church would finally close its doors.

Thomas looked from the chancel where he stood among the choristers. He could see the organist/choir master in the loft, conducting the musicians when he had a free hand from the keys. The notes rose into the wrought-iron fixtures and echoed in the stucco ceiling. "Forever, and ever, Hallelujah, Hallelujah! Hal—lay—you-ya!" The sparse numbers didn't have the strength to compete with the organ or the orchestra and their voices were drowned. Then there was silence.

Thomas looked down at the pew where his family sat. His mother and grandmother were smiling. His father snapped a picture on his Kodak Pony, and his grandfather was weeping. As the family gathered in the narthex to help Thomas into his coat, the boy looked at his grandfather and wanted to know if the old man had heard anything. The old man understood and nodded.

"I saw every word you sang," he told Thomas. "That's the way prayers are received. We are always too far away to be heard."

Sheet Music

HE COULD SEE his father's fists tighten as his grandmother told the story over Sunday dinner. His mother knew the story was upsetting because she had heard the truth behind it from one of his cousins and dreaded the day the events would be recounted at a family gathering. From where he sat, the boy saw his father's white knuckles and the blood pink skin between the bones in his father's hands. He knew from experience what rage looked like on the man.

"Oh, it was terrible," his maternal grandmother said as she bowed her head. "The lists would come out daily in the morning papers, the telegram boys would round the corners of streets and you'd try to remember who lived there and if he had danced with you. Everyone lived in fear. The lists of wounded were more encouraging though the scant information left one wondering if someone had lost an arm or an eye. As much as it troubled the imagination, 'wounded' meant there was some hope. Surely, the wounded would recover and come home. To be missing was worse than death. Not hearing anything meant next day would also be a living hell. Imagine, four years of that."

She cut three green beans and pierced them with her

fork, then set down the cutlery and continued. "I was working in the bank. They'd run short of men, and a woman who had book-keeping experience was just what they needed." She picked up the silver gravy boat at her right hand and garnished her potatoes. "Mr. Walker was the manager at my branch of the Dominion Bank. He had an only son. He was so proud of that boy. And then, one morning, I went in to open my till and there was a 'Bank Closed Today' sign in the window. That was never supposed to happen. The bank had to stay open no matter what. It was our job to keep it open. That's when I found him with his arm crooked on the top of his desk, weeping. I asked him what was wrong and Mr. Walker, still clutching the telegram, said: 'Oh! He's been killed. His mother doesn't know, but he's gone. Those damned Germans. I will make them pay for what they've done. I will make them pay in blood.'"

The boy's father cleared his throat, then said: "He surely did make them pay." The grandmother stared at the boy's father. They looked at each other in silence as the clock on the sideboard struck a single chime to mark the half hour. To the boy, the note sounded discordant as if time was complaining about something that should have been forgotten, but the boy could tell as the gears turned and the inner cogs clunked to reset the chime that something more than the clock was chewing itself from the inside.

The war had been years and years ago, the boy thought as his grandmother and grandfather stood at the kitchen sink, washing up the dishes. His father sat in the living room with his head in his hands, and his eyes visibly red with tears he kept trying to hide. As the boy looked at his father, his father stood up. "I never want you to see me crying, not now or ever again."

"So, why are you crying?" the boy asked.

His father moved toward the window to stare at the leaves that were falling from the red maple on the boulevard, and then turned to the boy. "Hate is a terrible thing. Hate is what ruined my family."

The boy's mother intervened. "Ssh," she said, trying to calm her husband.

"What do you mean, Dad?"

"No, don't go into it here," the boy's mother said.

"Your other grandfather ran a business. He spoke German to his employees. He loved to drink pilsner. Pilsner! He thought that put him in touch with his roots. He wasn't even from Germany. He was from the States. His father had been German, but it was who he was, and he had every right to be who he was—your other grandfather, my father—the one you never met. He had a business—a small motor company that made gas engines for appliances and such. He built his business up from nothing. When the Crash came, the banker called in his loan even though he had enough money to repay it and offered to repay it. The banker called your grandfather into his office and said: 'No German bastard is going to use my bank's money to build engines for war machines!' This was eleven years after the war ended. It ruined my father. It ruined me. We lost all our money. We lost our house. I spent the rest of my childhood bottling lubricating oil in the basement of a rented house—oil for engines we couldn't make anymore. The banker was that Walker."

The boy's father choked up and said no more. The boy's mother, shuddered, and heard her mother moving from the kitchen to the dining room. In an act of desperation to mask the tension in the living room, she sat down at the piano, thumbed through the sheet music, and started to play her favourite, Brahms' *Waltz in B Flat*.

"Really," her mother said, settling herself on the chesterfield as the boy's father, turned around again, and stared out the front window. "That's Brahms. I never liked him. He's German, isn't he? Play something French. See if *Salut D'Amour* is in the stack of music. That's a good thing. Play something English."

Gift

SHE HAD NO idea why her family had given her the name of a legendary detective company. The sound of her name, especially in the middle grades when students became aware of the historic connotations of her first and surname, triggered titters in the class when a supply teacher took attendance. She was teased at recess. Other kids asked her what she was guarding. They pressed her against walls and demanded she share the combination to an imaginary safe. She did her best to ignore them, but it hurt. Her regular teachers, after much pleading on her part, called her Pink for short.

The name Pinkerton, her family told her, was something she should be proud of. She had a right to her name, not just any name, and no one, not school bullies nor mean girls who raged against anything outside of their limited sense of the usual who pretended to be her friends and weren't, could take that from her. It was a name that had been her great, great, grandmother's.

That woman from the past who had gifted her name to Pink had a father who owed some sort of debt of life or property salvation the secret service men who were supposed to guard Abraham Lincoln and did a good job except for the one

April night at the Ford Theatre. She wondered if her namesake ancestor had been a Northern spy, disguised as a cunning southern belle, a woman of apparent means who knew how to play a hand of poker, held her liquor, and practiced espionage while smoking a cigar. Despite the taunts and jibes from her classmates, Pinkerton was a name she could live with. It was her ancestral name that gave her the most trouble.

That ancestor, Harold Present, had come to the city as an impoverished farm boy from Sweden. Present is not considered a Swedish name. There was always speculation among Pink's family that his real name may have been Persson or Presensson, and that it became corrupted by nineteenth-century census-takers who had notoriously bad ears when dealing with people who spoke accented English. Another theory offered by the family was that a roll call had been taken on Harold's arrival in Halifax, and that he had simply put up his hand when his name, or a version thereof had been called, and declared himself "Present." Whatever the case, the name stuck.

Pink was Pinkerton from her mother's side and Present on her father's side. There was a Mackenzie in the class, a girl whose first name was a clan name, and Pink liked to point out that last names were perfectly acceptable as first ones. That settled matters until Pink reached junior high school and had a locker next to Jessica Smith.

Jessica, Pink later learned, was not the girl's real name. When a class list fell from a teacher's desk and Pink did the teacher the courtesy of picking it up, she realized Jessica was a *nom de plume*, a pseudonym, and her real name was Jane. Jane Smith. Pink thought nothing of it other than to feel that Jessica's bullying—the dumping of her books on the crowded staircases, the cockroach Jessica tucked in Pink's sandwich, the powdered cleanser in her gym togs—was an over-compensation for someone who was hiding something. What made matters worse was that Jessica teased Pink about guarding some terrible gift.

"After all," Jessica said, "your name suggests you are guarding the Crown Jewels or something. You're hiding something! Hey, everyone, what is Pink hiding? If you have a present you'd better have one for everyone." The torments from the bully continued. Pink asked her parents if she could move to another school. Her parents told her that she had to be brave, that it wasn't the first time their name had been the target of jest and probably not the last either.

Pink lay awake for nights trying to think of what she could do to get even with Jessica, in a nice, polite way without seeming to get even, without giving the appearance of being mean in the face of someone else's meanness.

She had read, in English class, a book of Greek Mythology and became fascinated by the story of the Trojan Horse.

That is when the idea came to her.

The next day, Pink went to the stationer's store at the mall and bought a gift box and the most expensive paper and ribbon she could afford. She wrapped the box with neat, folded lines, and set the bow on top. She would present Jessica with a gift, a peace offering, but only on the condition that Jessica not open it in front of the other girls. Pink's terms were spelled out on the floral gift card she attached to the package, a card that listed the virtues of having someone like Jessica as a dear friend.

The girls at the lunch table were playing euchre. They sat with their cards pressed against their chests with one hand

and their sandwiches in the other. Pink asked if she could join them. Most of the girls shrugged. They didn't care one way or another, and one girl, Ann, went so far as to suggest they might deal her in after the hand they were playing.

Jessica said no.

Then, she reached over and knocked Pink's sandwich on the floor. The bread opened and the meat lay on the dirty tiles.

Pink looked at Jessica and smiled.

The other girls stared in disbelief, one whispering behind her hand of cards that maybe they were finally going to have the knock-down, drag-em-out fight everyone had anticipated.

Pink simply nodded and kept smiling. Then she handed Jessica the gift bag with the package in it. "I got you something, something I know you will want to own, something you probably already have but have forgotten how to use. But you mustn't open it in front of everyone. It is a peace offering between me and you. I really do want us to be friends, so please accept this in the spirit in which it is given. And don't open it now."

Jessica glared at Pink, then tore off the paper.

"There is nothing you can give me, you cow, no crap you can shove in my face that would make me stop loathing you or your ugly name." The other girls were silent. Pink sat with her hands folded in her lap.

Inside the box, among the tissue paper, was an envelope, and on the front of the envelope was an inscription: "For Jessica, my special friend—please don't share this with anyone." Jessica immediately tore the envelope open and pulled out a small piece of paper. She stared at the paper, and then crumpled it into the palm of her hand. She stood up, glared at Pink, and began to cry, then ran sobbing from the cafeteria.

"What did you say to make her do that?" Ann asked.

Pink shrugged. "I simply told her I forgave her, and that I wanted to be her friend and that we would share some wonderfully guarded secrets with each other such as the magical meanings of our names."

Toll

Two bells summoned the children of our street—one they liked and the other they found fascinating. The ice cream truck was famous. Mike, the scooper, had five flavours though only three on hot days because his fridges never worked well. The other was a brass bell.

The old man who rang the brass bell would never tell us his name and he spoke with a foreign accent as his foot pumped the treadle and sparks flew from his grindstone. Our mothers relied on his infrequent appearances. The grinder rang his bell and pulled the stone behind him on a wooden cart when he was tired and pushed it uphill when he turned the corner onto the next street. We would ask to ring the bell, but he always said no.

McBride's great-grandmother had pared her favourite blade down to a fish-knife, but its second life as a de-boner saved the implement from the trash. The pointed tip was sensitive to the smallest salmon vertebrae because McBride's mother understood that knives, like everything else, can do unexpected things.

Everyone liked McBride. He was always involved in whatever we were doing—the first one out on the street for road hockey, the last one to come in. What was more, he owned one of the nets, so he had to be part of things. He wasn't a bad goalie, and in the summer, when our street turned dusty and games relocated to the local diamond where we played baseball instead, he was a pretty good catcher though his throws to second were always slow.

McBride's mother had been on the phone when the grinder walked by, clanging his grinder's brass bell like a teacher in a school yard to scold scufflers. It rang with every third step the grinder took. The grinder was walking faster than usual, perhaps because he disliked the kids gathering round, or perhaps because he had to be somewhere at the end of his daily grind. McBride's mother called to him to catch the knife man before he turned onto the next block, and running back to his front porch, she handed McBride the old, dulled blade.

The next day the teacher rang her recess bell—a brass dome with a worn black wooden handle—and everyone lined up at the double doors as usual. When the Principal appeared instead of letting us in, we knew what was going to be said. We knew he was going to tell us that running with a knife can be lethal.

Seeing the boy writhe in agony on the sidewalk, the grinder decided not to stick around and simply walked away. When he turned the corner onto the next street, his bell began to toll again.

Tentacle

ONE OF THE beach-goers ran to get a bottle of Windex from his car. The boy's screams were softer by the time the man returned and poured what he had left of the blue liquid on the angry red welts.

The tentacle had left a pattern around the boy's torso. His chest heaved, and he coughed. He might have been coughing up salt water, but he hadn't drowned. Most people know what to do with drowning victims. They push out the water and breathe into the lungs. But this was different. This boy had been stung.

A policeman arrived and stood over the boy, cradling the child's head in his hand, asking: "Where are your parents?" And looking up anxiously in the hope they might appear. Those in the crowd looked over their shoulders for someone to arrive, but no one came to claim the child.

Neville stood and watched.

He tried to speak up, to tell the officer that Gary's parents were at their cottage, and that it wasn't far away, but he didn't know where, exactly. His words were drowned out by the policeman.

The officer shouted: "Everyone back. Give the kid some

air." He lifted a walk-talkie to his mouth and said: "What's the ETA on the ambulance?"

A stout, hairy-chested man whose belly protruded over the top of his swim trunks spoke up. "I pulled him in. I don't know who he is."

Gary gasped, and his eyes went wide. The policeman picked up the stricken boy and carried him in his arms to the public parking lot. Neville stood still, turned, and watched the sunlight sparkling on the low waves.

Three days before the tentacle attached itself to the stricken boy, Neville had met Gary on the beach. It was low-tide. The water was shallow and almost dead calm in the fog. They struck up a conversation.

Neville admired Gary's mask and snorkel and said he wished he had one too.

Gary had told him that he'd spotted pirate's treasure just off shore about twenty yards.

"It is deep there," Neville said, half to warn, and half inspired by Gary's courage. They had climbed out to the end of the black break wall rocks the beach authority installed to keep the sand from eroding. They peered between the boulders at the periwinkles. Gary tried to scrape some of them off because he said they were a nuisance.

"They just cling to things and don't do nothing else."

As the ambulance pulled away, Neville picked up the mask and snorkel Gary had left behind.

The policeman approached and stood where Gary had been laid on the sand. He pulled out a notebook and began to write. The hairy chested man gave his name.

"My name is Neville," the boy said to the policeman, clutching the mask and snorkel tightly by the straps.

"Don't need yours son. You're a minor. Run along, now. And stay out of the water. I'm having a sign posted today. It's man'o war season."

Neville wondered what a man'o war was. He pictured a galleon. Maybe it was the one returning to find the lost treasure Gary had spotted.

He sat down on the sand and stared at the ocean.

It was too beautiful to be off limits, and he only had a few days more left in his vacation. The waters were sparkling. Neville imagined each pinpoint of light as the soul of a drowned pirate signalling for help by flashing a doubloon in the sun.

Bicycle Bell

UNCLE THOMAS TOLD me never to ring my bicycle bell as I approached someone's house. It was a sign of ill omen. "Best to be a shadow and come and go," he said.

I had a paper route. When he was young, and sold *The Telegram* on a street corner instead of having a door to door paper route, all he had to do was hold up a copy. But because I had to deliver the news door to door, Uncle Thomas showed me how to roll up the paper into a log and tuck the edges together as if I was settling the hands of a corpse in a final clasp. But Uncle Thomas gave up being a newsy and became a telegram boy for Canadian Pacific. The money was better. "Newsies had it rough," he said, as he puffed on his pipe and stared at the back garden.

Every now and then, he'd nod at some imaginary person who stood beside the fence or bent over the flower bed. In the good weather, I'd join him on the wooden steps, and he'd offer random bits of wisdom, and tell me to remember what he said. I can't remember most of it, but one of the things he said most often and shake his head with a "no" was: "You never want to be the bearer of bad news."

When my grandmother and Uncle Thomas were out one

day, I found the family album in its hiding place in the dining room sideboard. I came across a snapshot of Uncle Thomas in his navy-blue uniform with brass buttons down the front. He wore a French policeman's hat. The hat had a shiny black peak. He had a leather bag slung over his shoulder. He was standing next to his bicycle. Uncle Thomas never married, and by the time I was a boy in the early Sixties, he'd grown hard of breathing, as he put it, from smoking a pipe he fancied. That night I thought I would ask him about it, about what the city was like back then. He must have known it well, riding up and down its streets, searching out addresses and bringing his news to every nook and cranny.

Uncle Thomas was smoking his pipe and let me have a drag on it. He said I was old enough. I was ten. I told him it tasted bitter, and it did—the sour mouthpiece, and acrid smoke. "It's all bitter," he replied, taking the pipe back. He stared at the flower bed for several minutes. He looked at me as if I was asking too much. Maybe I was. Then he tapped his pipe on the steps and the ashes fell between the treads.

"One day I had to bring three telegrams to a woman." He paused. "That was the worst day of my life. People hated the sight of the telegram boy. I was the angel of death. The woman of the house opened the envelopes, opened them slowly, one by one—one for her husband and two for her boys—and I think she hoped at least one message would say that one of them was wounded and might come back to her. She sank down on the doorstep and clutched my arm so tight I had black bruises from her fingertips. She wept for a few minutes, and then fell silent. I got up to leave, and she pulled me back down. 'Please don't leave,' she repeated until her words became a whisper. So, I sat there with her, our feet sticking out the door, splayed in front of us. We just sat in silence. I have never been able to hear wind through leaves since then as merely wind through leaves. I heard it as the silence of a broken heart."

"What happened next?" I asked.

"We sat there all day. Night fell. Stars appeared through the boughs of the maples. She put her head against my shoulder and eventually she fell asleep, so I picked her up as best I could and carried her to the settee in her parlor. When I got back to the depot, I was docked a day's pay. The chief clerk said I'd be sacked if it happened again, that I was slacking off, and had to mend my ways. I wish I could have mended more, I told him, but world doesn't work that way."

Then, Uncle Thomas pointed with the stem of his pipe toward the flower bed.

"Your grandfather planted roses there. Your uncle Jimmy and your Uncle Michael were prize-winning gardeners, too. I can still see them standing there, turning over the earth as if they were trying to find a shred of beauty in the muck, as if they were looking for the life they were certain that was down in the ground. All my life I've been looking for it, too, and never found it. I should have been better at what I did. I've never known what to say, never found the words to say it. I've been the shadow at the door. But the one day I needed to be professional, the one day I needed to be the perfect telegram boy, I wasn't. I spent the better part of my life walking up to doors, handing people news, some of it good but most of it bad, and the hardest path I ever had to walk was the one to the front door of this house as I handed the telegrams to my mother."

The Fishers

HIS GRANDSON WAS five now, the age at which the old man had been taught to fish by his grandfather. The finest fishing places where the grandfather had first cast his lines were far to the south, so close to the city that they had been swallowed by subdivisions and the overlay of streets. Streams where the trout once ran were now buried as sewer lines to catch the run-off from house farms where dwellings ran in repetitive ranks, some on curving crescents and others on straight avenues. The best creeks had dried up. The world was dying before his eyes. It wasn't fair that this should happen. Instead of fighting progress, the old man decided to head north beyond the reach of change and teach his grandson the beauty and stillness of fishing.

Sunlight was sparkling on the tea-coloured river. A woman with a kind face had told them they could use her landing dock for casting their lines. She said the fish liked to gather on summer mornings beneath a pod of willows on the far shore, though that had been some time ago, and she warned they might not catch anything no matter how long they waited. Her husband hadn't caught anything there in ten years. She said it was not because he hadn't taken the time to sit still and drop his line; it was just the changes in the water.

The old man was certain he could prove her wrong. There'd been a lot of rain in the past week and the water levels were high, but the current tailed off to a lazy drift. Cool and slow in the sunlight. He told his grandson how fish like to shelter in the shadows.

The dock sat low in the water. It leaned to one side where a broken gunnel was submerged, and the boy took the old man's hand as they carefully walked around the wet portion of the slanted platform. Orange moss was growing on the boards. The old man sat down and removed his shoes and socks and set them behind him beside the tackle box so he could let his toes and ankles feel the current. The boy wasn't sure he wanted to remove his runners.

"It isn't cold," the old man said.

He nestled the boy to the other side of him. The child held up his feet, one at a time, and reached around behind the old man to set his empty runners and short navy socks beside his grandfather's.

"There we go," the old man said. "Side by side, and foot by foot."

After feeding the hook with a worm from a Mason jar—something that troubled the boy who asked if the worm felt pain to which the old man shook his head, "No," they dropped their lines in the river. The red and white floats bobbed, and the lead sinkers held the hook end of the lines taut.

"Now we just sit and wait for something to happen."

"What do we think about?" the boy asked.

"Anything you want. Fishing is not about catching fish as it is about sitting here, dreaming whatever you want to dream, and waiting quietly for the sun to climb over our shoulders and settle on the far bank among the trees. That's when it will be time to call it a day."

The old man could hear the current moving softly downstream and could feel the flow as it ran cool between his toes. A leaf floated by. Later, a branch broken from a tree upstream drifted past. The boy shut his eyes and turned his face to the sun.

Would his grandson remember this day years from now when, perhaps, with a grandchild of his own, he would share the patient pleasure of being a fisher? So many moments, so much sadness, and sometimes joy, too, had converged to bring them there. And for one instant, the old man wanted time to cease—the river, the calm stillness in the trees, his grandson, and even himself—and all the people and places and things worth loving in the world to live forever.

Acknowledgements

Some of the stories in this book have appeared in literary magazines and zines in Canada, the United States, and Great Britain. The author is grateful to the editors for their support and encouragement.

"Cadenza," appeared on *Fictive Dream* zine (USA).

"Consuelo" appeared in *Reflex Fiction* (UK).

"Toll" and "Alabaster" placed fourth and fifth respectively in the *London Independent Short Fiction Prize* and were published on the prize's website (UK).

"What Kasha Said," appeared in *Parhelion Literary Magazine* (USA).

"Edible Flowers," appeared in the anthology *Heat the Grease*, published by Gnashing Teeth Press (USA).

"Popcorn," "Bicycle Bell," and "Monster," appeared on *Story Pub* (UK).

"The Sophomore Philosophy Club," appeared on *Half a Grapefruit* (Toronto).

"Sadness," won fourth prize in the Bath Short Story Prize (UK) and appeared in the *Bath Short Story Prize Anthology, 2019*.

"Ear to the Ground," appeared on *Blue Nib* (US).

"Warts" appeared in *The Blake Jones Review* (Canada) and received the second-place prize in their annual fiction competition.

The author is grateful to the Ontario Arts Council and its Recommender Grants Program for their gracious support. The funds helped bring this project to completion. The grants received were from Exile Editions, Black Moss Press, Guernica Editions, Insomniac Press, *The New Quarterly*, and The Porcupine's Quill. Many thanks to Tim and Elke Inkster, Marty Gervais, Michael Callaghan, Michael Mirolla, and Mike O'Connor for their recommendations.

The author wishes to thank Michael Mirolla for his editorial insights and feedback, David Moratto for his excellent design, Anna Van Valkenberg for her tireless promotion of this and my other Guernica Editions books, Trasie Sands, Dave Gregory, Antonia Facciponte and Benjamin Berman Ghan for their helpful suggestions as I talked through some of the challenges of these stories, Aaron Reynolds and Linda Laforge of *Word Up*, Barrie for permitting me to road-test some of these stories in front of a live audience, Dr. Carolyn Meyer and Margaret Meyer for their continued enthusiasm, and Katie Meyer and Kerry Johnston for their unending love and support.

About the Author

Bruce Meyer is author or editor of sixty-four books of poetry, short fiction, flash fiction, nonfiction, and literary journalism. His most recent books are *McLuhan's Canary* (poems), *A Feast of Brief Hopes* (short stories) from Guernica Editions. His *Portraits of Canadian Writers* was a national bestseller in 2016, and his broadcasts on the CBC on *The Great Books, A Novel Idea*, and *Great Poetry* with Michael Enright remain the network's bestselling spoken word audio series. He was winner of the Anton Chekhov Short Story Prize for 2019, and short listed for the Strand International Fiction Prize 2019, The London Independent Short Story Prize 2019, the Retreat West Short Story Prize 2020, Tom Gallon Trust Fiction Prize 2019, the Carter V. Cooper Prize in 2019, and the Bath Short Story Prize in 2019. He lives in Barrie, Ontario and was inaugural Poet Laureate for that city.